THE PREVIOUS ADVENTURES OF...

By

MARY LAY

The characters in this book are fictitious, although some factual events and locations have been referred to. Any similarity to actual persons, living or dead, is coincidental.

ISBN 978-1-7396653-6-4 (e-book)
ISBN 978-1-7396653-7-1 (paperback)

First edition July 2023

Independently published by Mary Lay Stories www.marylaystories.com

Formatting by Eryn McConnell

Also by Mary Lay

Catching Up
The Price of Coal
Birds of the Storm

For my dearest friend Ciel, who gave me courage.

CONTENTS

FOREWORD

This collection of short stories is an attempt to appease some of the characters from my *Catching Up* series of novels. Those characters, some minor and some less so, had more to say than I had allowed them in the novels. Social history fascinates me; the lives of every-day people are so rich, so full of twists and turns, of what ifs and should haves. The characters wanted to tell their stories alongside Caroline.

If you've not read the series, perhaps they might interest you enough to tempt you to. If you have, I hope these give some extra background without distracting you from Caroline's on-going exploration of the world she finds herself in.

There is, no doubt, more to come from all of them.

Mary Lay, 2023.

BETTY AND THE SUFFRAGETTES

THE WHITE DRESS ON the coat hanger needed a wash. Betty had made it herself out of two old bedsheets, as having to purchase a new dress for her activities was out of the question on her wages from the laundry. After covering her room and board for the week, she had less than three shillings and most of that had to go on tram fares. Not for the first time, Betty wondered if she shou ld H have stayed with her old employer and not walked out.

Being in service at least meant she had food, somewhere to sleep and clothes on her back, even if it also meant long hours, chapped and sore hands, and the unwanted attentions of the under-butler. He had been the reason Betty had left, very early one March morning in 1907. Now she worked a late shift, six days a week, ironing linens for hotels and wealthy houses.

Betty would have given her right little finger if it meant she could have stayed at school. That honour had gone to her brother Robert. Younger by 18 months, Robert was doing well, her father's short letters reported. He was showing an aptitude at numbers and their father hoped he might become an engineer.

Betty wondered if her father had ever had such aspirations for her, beyond marrying her off into a family with more than a few farthings left at the end of each week. She doubted it. Being born a girl had consigned her to going into service as soon as position could be found when she turned twelve, no matter that she was as good at maths as Robert and could read and write too.

That felt a lifetime away now. Betty looked at her reflection in the hand mirror she kept on top of the small chest of drawers in her room. Five years had changed her; sometimes she hardly recognised herself.

There was a gentle knock on the door. Emma poked her head through the gap between the door and frame.

"Are you ready?"

Betty picked up the man's overcoat from her bed. "Yes. Let's go."

They were dressed as working-class men, with their long hair tucked and pinned up underneath flat caps. The freedom of simply wearing trousers was liberation itself, but the young women had greater things on their minds as they walked quickly through the streets of central London.

Betty was glad of the overcoat. They had expected rain, it being October, but not the cold wind that blasted them around every corner as they got closer to Westminster. They had discussed the possibility of arriving by tram but decided the risk of being questioned as to why they were wearing men's clothes should be avoided at all costs. They were only convincing at a distance.

As they reached Caxton House, their appointed meeting place, there was already a throng of people moving towards the river. Betty spotted Celia, Jemima and Jenny despite their male garb, and nudged Emma. It was still early. Betty wondered if they would be able to get to the front of the protest if this many people were already on their way there.

"Do you have the banner?" Emma asked Jenny. There were no polite greetings, this was serious business. Jenny nodded, opening her overcoat a little to show the corner of a calico sheet folded inside.

"And the leaflets." Added Jemima. She was a veteran of the movement and older than the others by five or six years. Widowed and having spent some time in the poorhouse, she had been prostituting herself when Jenny had found her under a canal bridge and taken her home. Once Jemima's bruises had faded, Jenny took her to work at the laundry. They had been inseparable ever since.

"Last chance to turn around and go home." Emma watched each of the women's faces. They were set with determination. "Celia are you absolutely sure about this? Who is watching Aveline?"

"Mother has her, she is perfectly safe, and I am perfectly sure."

"Come on then."

The women joined the hoard of bodies moving through Broad Sanctuary and into the grassy space outside the House of Commons.

Not every woman had arrived in men's attire. Plenty of wide-brimmed hats could be seen across the sea of bodies. Some of the supporters of the movement were men in any case; though they were vilified by their fellow sex, they sought universal suffrage. Those women who had attempted to disguise themselves however soon found each other in the melee and banded together as they so often had before. As the crowd grew, chanting began.

"It's the 'jists'," Jemima muttered, craning her neck to see over the heads and hats around her.

"They won't get in our way. They never do." Emma's voice was cold and low. She meant to get as close to the railings as possible and if she could, handcuff herself to them. The restraints were in her pocket, stolen by an accomplice the week before from an unsuspecting policeman. Emma did not have the key; she would have to be cut out.

"Is that Helen Fox?" Betty was looking in the opposite direction at a small group of women dressed as she and her friends were who marched determinedly forwards.

"Yes! And Alison Noilans too. Come on, let's follow them, they'll be in the thick of things." Celia's eyes were wide with admiration, and she pulled at Betty's sleeve.

The women picked up speed, pushing and shoving their way through the tightening crowd. Everyone was tense, different factions chanting over the top of each other, a general din of unease and anger. Some were singing *The March of the Women*.

Agitators were heckling the women from the outer edges and throwing potatoes. Some groups held up trade union banners. There was a small knot of Salvation Army members in uniform, singing to a fiddle and tambourine. When the word 'Forward!' rang out, suddenly the crowd moved *en mass*, stepping one way then pushing back another as if caught in a murmuration of starlings.

Betty reached out for Emma, but she was swept to Betty's left and away with the crowd. Betty looked to her right and saw Celia now three rows back and reaching over the shoulders of those in front of her towards Betty. Then Celia disappeared from sight.

As the crowd shifted again, Betty almost lost her balance. Grasping hold of the coat in front of her, she managed to stay on her feet. The owner turned sharply and scowled at her. Though the weather was cold, the tight press of bodies and the growing fear Betty felt caused sweat to break out on her brow and back. Instinctively she turned back towards where she had last seen Celia. Those behind her swore at her, shoved and tried to turn her around again, but she battled back through the bodies, elbowing, stamping and calling out Celia's name.

Twenty feet across and then five bodies deep Betty fought. Suddenly the crowd opened; Celia was sitting on the damp street, a young man in a flat cap and rough clothes was bent over next to her trying to hold back the press of humanity from trampling them both.

Celia looked up at Betty, "I fell, I think my finger is broken and I hit my head on something..."

"Come on, up you get, we need to get out of here."

Betty pulled Celia to her feet and with the help of the man, elbowed their way further from the railings around the Houses of Parliament and the growing phalanx of policemen. It took some minutes for them to gain enough space to pause; by that time, they were almost back at the Sanctuary. People were still streaming towards the Commons, but the trio were able to step to the side of the flow and catch their breath.

"Let me see your hand, Celia." Betty held out her own.

The top of Celia's little finger bent at an unnatural angle and the joint was already discoloured. She could feel a graze on her elbow, and something was trickling down the side of her neck. Celia reached up with her other hand and and brought away blood from her skin.

"Oh Lord. I did hit something!" She swayed and turned a pale grey.

"Steady now!" The young man grabbed her shoulders and moved her further back on the pavement, pushing her to sit down again.

On inspection, Betty located the cut just above Celia's ear and did her best to clean the wound and stem the flow of blood with her handkerchief. As she worked, the blast of whistles filled the air and shouts went up that drowned the chanting and singing of the crowds.

"Can you walk?" The man asked. There was a hint of an accent in his voice.

"I think so, if you could help me up again." Celia tried to smile at her helper.

"We can manage from here," Betty asserted, as Celia was again hoisted upright.

She looked at the man properly for the first time. He was as tall as she was, red hair cut short and a day's growth of red beard on his chin. His clothes were worn, the rough working outfit that so many men wore, but he had a red neckerchief instead of a collar and tie. His cap was grey and sat pulled down at the front, so that he looked up from under the brim almost sideways.

"I'll see you out of the crowd. Which way do you need to go?"

Betty bit her lip. She did not like to give way to a man, but Celia still looked grey around the gills and the police whistles were getting closer. He also hadn't questioned their clothing.

"Alright, we need to get back to Fulham, we're not going to be able to get to Westminster station, so let's head for Victoria."

"You didn't have to, you know." Betty said for the sixth time since they had left Celia in the care of her mother.

"If we only did what we had to, where would be the joy in life?" Percy asked with a small smile.

They walked side by side towards Betty's lodgings, her plaited hair now uncoiled and hanging over her shoulder, the cap rolled up and pushed into a pocket in her overcoat. While half carrying Celia home, she had learned that Percy was Irish though he had lived in London for twenty of his twenty-three years. He had a belief that all men were equal and should be franchised as such, and this extended to women most of the time. The subject of universal suffrage had been a common one in his small community in Hammersmith, where most believed in no taxation without representation, particularly when it was the British government gathering the taxes.

Percy worked as a locksmith and attended night classes at the Working Men's Institute to hear more about social and political economics and to improve his writing.

When they reached the steps that led up to the front door of Betty's home, she stopped and held out her hand. "This is me, then. It was nice to meet you Percy, but I think I should be getting inside now. I've got to be at work in half an hour."

Percy looked at Betty's outstretched hand. He took it in his, shook it twice, then pulled Betty to him while stepping forward and kissed her full on the lips. Betty was too shocked to object. After a moment Percy stepped back again and let go of her hand.

"In my country, we'd be engaged to be married now, Betty Lewis. What do you say to that?"

"I say you're taking a bleedin' liberty Percy Chandler!" Betty wiped her mouth on the back of her hand, though mostly for show. She wouldn't have objected to another kiss, but she wasn't going to let Percy know that.

"You'll be going to the police court tomorrow, to see your friends?"

"If we can get inside. If not, we'll wait outside and see what the judgements are. I hope Emma is alright."

Betty had known of Emma's plan with the handcuffs but had not wanted to go as far as that. She was meant to be holding the banner alongside Jemima and Jenny. She hoped they had got close enough to the House to show it.

"I'll be here at ten o'clock then." Percy started to walk away sideways, smiling at Betty. "Votes for Women!" He shouted.

Betty raised her fist, "Votes for Women!" she replied. She was still watching him as he turned the corner at the end of the street.

Two weeks later, Percy and Betty sat in the Gaumont Cinema, waiting for the newsreel to begin. Betty hadn't had time to go home and change out of her white dress, but she had kept the man's overcoat and now pulled it a little tighter around her.

"How did she look?" Percy asked as he removed his cap.

"Christabel? Like she hadn't eaten for a week. I thought there would be more from the Movement there, but only ten or so turned up to welcome her back."

"And your friend Emma gets out next week?"

"Unless she does something else while she's in there. She kicked a policeman, I'm sure she'd not baulk at doing the same to a warder."

Percy took Betty's hand. "It's an important cause, but I'm glad you didn't get yourself arrested, my girl."

"I suppose we have Celia's broken finger to thank."

"How is she?"

"Oh, she's alright. It's Jenny I'm more worried about. Her Jack gave her a black eye for getting involved when she got home. He's about ready to throw Jemima out, I think. He says she's filling Jenny's head with ideas above her station."

"Some men don't see it as a means to an end. I don't know why. Maybe because they haven't had to pick mouldy potatoes out of someone else's rubbish heap for their dinner. I heard there was more trouble over Shoreditch way a couple of nights ago. Bricks through windows. Pillar boxes set fire to. You didn't have anything to do with that, did you?"

"Shhhh! Keep your voice down. No, I didn't. I've been at work every night, you're lucky I'm here tonight. Emma is taking my shift so I can see you, and I've got to do hers on Saturday, so you'll have to entertain yourself."

"I've got a spot of business to take care of on Saturday. The Latvians have come across the river again. I thought they'd have learned after Stepney, but seems they can't keep their hands to themselves. Oh, and Patrick Moynaghan's sister Faith was arrested yesterday trying to chain up the signals outside Harringay station."

Betty gave Percy's hand a squeeze. "It won't always be so bad, I'm sure of it. There are so many more workers than the wealthy, they need us. Something will give eventually."

"That's my girl." Percy smiled. "Do you have any of those liquorice drops?"

CHANCE ENCOUNTER

"God bless you."

Philip Rose stood by the open coffin for a moment in silence before turning away and untying his apron. He lifted it over his head, hung it on the peg next to the door of the cluttered room, and exchanged it for his jacket and hat. Philip turned out the light and closed the door behind him.

The smell of the embalming room had never troubled him. The delicate procedures of washing, dressing and preparing a body for viewing and later for burial felt as natural to Philip as his own morning walks along the river or brushing his own teeth.

In taking care of the dead, Philip felt closest to God. It was his calling and had been for as long as he could remember; all through Technical College where he had studied the sciences, during his years working here at the undertakers, and then through his time at the Theology College, his faith and conviction had been unwavering.

"All done for tonight?" Albert looked up from the newspaper he was reading at the kitchen table as Philip entered the room.

"Yes. It's been good to see you again, Albert. I've often missed the old times here."

"Been good to have you back, even for a few days, lad. You know you're always welcome. Never a shortage of bodies need taking care of."

"And who is taking care of you Albert?" Philip asked gently. He had seen Albert struggle with the bottle lids and finer tools of the trade during his week-long stay.

Albert sniffed. "The Good Lord takes care of me. If I need help, he'll provide it, just as he did bringing you back for a few days, eh?"

His brow furrowed as he looked up at Philip."You've given so many years of service Albert, I'm sure Reverend Althorpe would be able to nominate you for one of the Alms-houses on Pennyroyal Street. It would be prudent to be on the waiting list sooner rather than later, don't you think?"

"I don't want no charity." Grumbled Albert.

"Of course not," Philip's voice was quiet, soothing, "Think of it as an investment that has seen a handsome return. When you are ready, when Randall is ready to take on the business completely here, it would be better if you were close to the top of the list, surely?"

"Randall would have it all now if I let him." Albert sat up straight in his chair.

"I'll think on it, young Philip. Now you be getting along home. Don't want to miss your train in the morning on account of sleeping late!"

Philip walked the dark silent streets of Nailsea back to his parents' house in contemplation. The next morning would see him head across the city to the church of Saint Agnes in the Saint Paul Diocese to begin his curacy. He was excited for his new opportunity, but equally sad to be leaving his parents and the community he had grown up with behind again.

He was the last of his siblings to leave home, his three older brothers all spread out around the globe on various trade and diplomatic missions. His mission had always been of the spiritual kind. His father had also trained as a curate but then decided not to pursue a career in the church. He had taken up writing and had published many theological works. He had been a staunch supporter of Philip's vocation, as had Philip's mother, and both were as excited as Philip that he had secured a curacy in the city.

Saint Agnes was a bustling church nestled in a warren of streets. Developed in the previous century, St Paul's was dominated by the Dye Works and the endless terraced housing stretched out like arteries and veins carrying the workers to and from the pumping heart of the area. The smell of the chemicals and the effluent that poured into the river and canal tainted those who lived and worked there. Most were poor, despite working long hours. The children were begrudgingly sent to school now beyond their twelfth birthdays, though many skipped lessons and found occupation down at the dockyard where a white lie could get them a day's work and a few pennies.

This was where Philip made his home, in a spare room at the Vicarage until he could find somewhere that the church approved of. His first week saw him thrown in at the deep end as the incumbent Vicar had a dose of food poisoning and was unable to carry out his own duties. Philip rose to the challenge and by the end of his fourth day as curate, felt he must have met every inhabitant of the parish through the services, visits and other activities that took place at Saint Agnes.

Some weeks into his curacy, Philip had obtained a ticket to a recital at the Colston Hall in the city centre. He was a member of the Bristol Temperance Progressionist Society, whose choir was to give the performance. The evening was cool with a slight mist rising from the river.

Philip walked with purpose and dropped a penny into the tin cup held out by a collection of rags and humanity on the steps that led up to River Street and into the city. He had been pleasantly surprised at how, since starting to wear his dog-collar and long black overcoat, people had treated him with a new level of respect and acknowledgement. He knew he looked young for his age and often had needed to speak up to gain attention in the past, but now he felt visible.

Philip was so enraptured by his new sense of being that he did not notice the the horse and carriage approaching as he stepped out to cross the street.

"No!"

A pair of stout black arms wound around his slender waist and pulled him back onto the path just in time. His hat was not so fortunate. Trampled under the horse's hooves, then almost dissected by the carriage wheels, it lay in tatters on the cobbles in front of him.

"You daydreaming, sir! Lord, but you would have been crushed. Good ting I saw you, yes indeed. Now, what have you to say for yourself?"

Philip was released from the wrestling hold, shaken but none the worse for his rescue. He turned and came face to face with a large black woman in a plain fawn-coloured dress, brown coat and a wide-brimmed felt hat that sported a paper flower on one side. She stood a couple of inches shorter than him, hands on hips, one stocking wrinkled at the ankle and deep brown eyes staring boldly into his own.

Celestine Vincent, previously of Trinidad and now resident of Bristol while her husband fought for King and country in Africa, was not a woman to be trifled with.

"I am so very sorry, madam..." Philip began.

Celestine noticed his dog collar. "A priest! Now I see. God made me an angel to save one of his own," she chuckled, her face softening and showing her white teeth.

"Well, I should have been looking where I was going. I am so very grateful for your assistance."

"I should tink so!" Celestine's smile vanished and she became stern again.

"Your hat, sir."

Philip turned back towards the road and looked into the dark eyes of a young girl, no more than seventeen or eighteen years old. He found his mouth suddenly dry. The girl dipped her eyes and waited for him to take the hat from her hand. "Thank you. Oh dear, it does rather look as though I shall have to buy another. This cannot be saved. How unfortunate. But you must let me thank you properly, Mrs...?"

"Vincent. Celestine Vincent. And my daughter Mary."

Celestine added with a raised eyebrow, noticing how Mary kept her eyes focused on Philip's shoes. "And you?"

"Philip Rose, I have just taken the curacy at Saint Agnes, and am on my way to a recital. Could I perhaps ask you to accompany me? By way of thanks?"

Celestine lifted her chin. "You asking us both?"

"Well, of course. Naturally. If you both enjoy choral music?"

Celestine nodded. She no more enjoyed choral music than swimming in the river Avon but she would not let any opportunity to be seen in society with a nice young vicar pass her by. She had Mary's future to think of, after all.

"We come."

Mary Vincent sat through the recital between her mother and the curate, acutely aware of where his arm, hip and thigh met hers. She would have preferred to sit on the other side of Celestine but had been too slow to engineer that arrangement. She found the singing pleasant though not overwhelmingly so. She joined in with the polite applause after each piece ended, and only then stole a glance at the young man next to her. His face animated with enjoyment, his features so perfectly arranged, she blushed each time and returned her gaze to the performers or her own knees.

Mary was not by nature a shy girl. Growing up in Bristol, in a small community of immigrants from various Caribbean islands, Ireland and across Europe, she had always been in the company of loud adults who expected her to hold her own. She would speak when spoken to, clear and confident, while watching the subtle changes in expression and interaction between those around her.

Celestine had arrived in Bristol with two-year-old Mary, with a single suitcase and five pounds in her pocket. Mary had been brought up in a boarding house with three other Caribbean families, never lacking for playmates though sometimes going to bed hungry while Celestine mended other people's clothes in the big kitchen below. She had gone to school and though she struggled with reading and writing, she excelled at mathematics. Numbers gave her a sense of order, knowing that there was always a single correct answer to the problems she was asked to solve.

When the time came for her to leave school, Mary's availability for employment was broadcast by Celestine to their community, along with Mary's ability to perform multiplication and long division. Through Tawny Antoine, family friend and man of charm and contacts, Mary took up a position as assistant to Moses Franks on a small fruit and vegetable stall in Saint Nicholas Market.

The work was hard with long hours, but everyone assumed Mary would have the strength to fulfil her duties and Moses appreciated another competent pair of eyes on his daily takings. There had been gossip, naturally, between the other market traders when Moses took on a black girl instead of any of the numerous war veterans. Younger men could earn more at the docks, and rarely wanted market work unless they had a family connection. Moses shrugged off the insinuations and instructed Mary to do the same. He paid her at the end of every day, openly in front of the nearest stall holders, to dispel any idea of slavery or impropriety.

Outside on the pavement after the recital, Philip hovered, not wanting to say goodbye without securing another meeting with the young girl.

"Will you be alright getting home?" he asked.

"Fine, fine. We not far to go from here."

"Thank you for the concert." Mary said, finally looking Philip straight in the eye.

"You are most welcome. Perhaps we could attend another? If it would be convenient for you?"

Celestine screwed up her nose. "I not hold with these tee-totallers!"

"Oh. Perhaps a moving picture then?"

"Saint Agnes, you say?" Celestine buttoned her coat.

Philip took a moment to catch up with the swerve in the conversation, still looking into Mary's eyes. "Oh, yes. Saint Agnes is where I am curate, yes."

"We shall see." Celestine declared. She pulled at Mary's arm and the two women walked off towards Saint Nicholas church leaving Philip gazing after them.

The following Sunday as Philip accompanied the Vicar from the vestry and took up his place near the font, Philip spotted a familiar brown felt hat with a paper flower and its owner sitting three pews back from the pulpit. Next to the owner of the hat, Mary Vincent held her head high and looked out across the congregation. She gave a slight smile as she saw Philip, which he returned.

After four Sundays in a row, Celestine was sufficiently content with her social engineering that she declared she would not be attending Saint Agnes again. Mary understood that now her progress was in her own hands, and the following Sunday she hung back as the rest of the congregation filed out of the church and bid the Vicar a good day. Philip was collecting the hymn books from the ends of the pews. Mary gathered the one she had used and the one left on the seat next to her and met him in the aisle.

"Thank you, Mary. Is your mother well?"

"Quite well, sir. She has decided she no longer needs to accompany me here."

Philip smiled at her lilting voice. It made him think of the sea lapping at the side of a boat. He had started to look forward to seeing Mary each Sunday, to exchange their small smiles and glances during the service. He realised he was falling in love. For her part, Mary liked the young curate but thought love was for older people. She was only just eighteen and had no immediate plans for her future. One day she hoped to have children and settle down somewhere in a little house, perhaps on the edge of the city. It all seemed a long way off. Yet she had decided to continue attending Saint Agnes each Sunday, when she had not been a regular attendee at Saint Nicholas' for years.

"If you can wait a few moments for me to change, perhaps I could walk with you back into the centre?" Philip took the two hymn books from Mary, their hands brushing against each other for a moment.

"I can wait."

"The young black woman?" The Vicar paused, his soup spoon halfway between his bowl and his mouth.

Philip put down his own spoon and dabbed his mouth with a napkin. Six months had passed since his rescue by Celestine, and his regular walks with Mary had convinced him that he wanted to marry her. Admittedly he was young, as was she, yet he was determined. He had spoken with his parents, who after some persuasion, had come round to the idea although they had not yet met Mary. Now he had to convince his employers: first the Vicar, then the Bishop.

"Mary Vincent, yes. I have my parent's blessing, though I have not yet asked Mary herself."

"And your parents are aware of her ... heritage?"

"I have explained that to them, yes. And that Mary's father is serving our country in Africa."

The Vicar took a mouthful of soup, swallowed, and continued, "Would Africa be of interest to you? There are opportunities for missionary work, which you might find suitable."

Philip had anticipated this. "Mary knows no other home than Bristol, she arrived here as a baby. We hope to find a parish in this country once I complete my curacy."

"Philip, I am not against this in principle. But have you fully considered how a congregation could react? It could make finding a parish particularly difficult."

"There are one or two other couples in Mary's neighbourhood where one is white and the other is black. We know in general people stay within their own kind, but we have become close and..."

"There is no immediate need for this?" The Vicar interrupted.

"No, not at all, nothing of that kind!" Philip blushed uncontrollably.

The Vicar relaxed a little and contemplated his soup once more. "Good, good. Wouldn't have been the first of course, but if you can avoid that sort of thing, then all the better for everyone. If there is no hurry, why not wait until you have your own parish? It would only be another three years, after all."

Philip picked up his spoon again but did not dip it into his soup. "I had hoped that we could be married next spring. If Mary accepts my proposal of course."

"And her parents agree also."

"Yes. I shall need to ask Celestine."

With the Vicar's consent, Philip asked Mary the following Sunday to be his wife. He had purchased a narrow gold band with a tiny diamond set in the centre, guessing the size of Mary's finger with an accuracy that disguised his nervousness of asking her. They had stopped by the riverside, with golden leaves drifting down around them and into the water. Mary had listened to Philip's proposal, her heart beating faster as she understood what he was asking of her. She hesitated, asked him if he was completely sure he knew what it could mean for them both. Only when he took her hands in his and kissed her there on the riverside did she agree.

They went together to tell Celestine. Philip had wanted to ask the older woman himself, but Mary insisted they do it together. They need not have worried. Celestine had been hoping for that day since she first met Philip and whooped with joy when she saw Mary's new ring. She brought out a bottle of rum and poured some into three teacups on her kitchen table before she remembered that Philip did not drink at all, and Mary rarely did. Instead, she made a pot of tea, and poured the rum into a single cup that she sipped from herself.

Their next challenge was an interview with the Bishop. Mary dressed with care and met Philip one Tuesday morning at College Green. It was raining and Mary's feet were already wet and splashed with mud from the uneven paving. She stood by the doors of the cathedral trying to keep out of the rain, watching for

Philip. He arrived, hopping off a tram just across the lawns and hurried towards her with his black umbrella bobbing as he jogged along. They kissed their greeting as Philip shook his umbrella, and then holding hands they entered the cool dark interior of the church.

Philip found the Deacon, who showed the couple through a side door and into a more modern building with a reception area and offices on the floor above. As the Bishop based himself at Winterbourne in north Gloucestershire, he used the offices and reception rooms for meetings when he was in the city. The Deacon returned after a few minutes and informed them that the Bishop would see Philip first. Mary was left by herself in the cold quiet room. She sat on the edge of a chair upholstered with a blue seat and back and looked at the portraits that lined the walls. White men looked down on her with various degrees of disinterest. She shivered. The Bishop could halt everything if he did not approve. Mary had already decided that if the Bishop said no to their marriage, she would break things off with Philip. She would not allow him to sacrifice his calling for her.

Thirty-five minutes passed as Mary waited in the reception room. No one offered her tea. Finally, the Deacon returned once more and asked Mary to follow him. He showed her into a smaller room where Philip and the Bishop were sitting opposite each other on two leather settees. The Bishop looked at her intently for a moment, appraising her as she had known so many other men to do while she worked in the market.

"Philip tells me your father is in the British Army. Where does he serve?"

The question was not what Mary had expected to be asked. She would have liked a sip of water, but there was none.

"In Nigeria, Your Grace."

"Excellent. And you were educated in Bristol?"

"Yes, Your Grace." She lifted her chin slightly and looked at him directly. "From school I have been employed by a grocer in Saint Nicholas." She did not elaborate that it was in the market, or that Moses was not a member of the Anglican church.

"Well, that will have to come to an end, of course."

The Bishop turned to Philip, leaving Mary standing across the room, and concluded their business. He stood, shook Philip's hand and wished them both a very happy future together.

After the Deacon had walked them back to the cathedral, Philip and Mary left and crossed College Green to take shelter in the Lyons' Corner House. As they waited for the Nippie to bring their tea and sandwiches, Philip reached across the table and took Mary's hand.

"Only my parents to meet now, Mary. They already know all about you, so it shouldn't be such an ordeal."

"The Bishop didn't have any objections at all?"

"Not once he knew your father is a soldier. I would never have guessed that information would be important, but it seemed to sway him. He did mention the option of missionary work – everyone appears to assume it is what we want to do. Yet when I explained we would be happier to find a small parish in the Diocese, he said that could be arranged. I rather think the Vicar has been fighting in our corner."

Moses was sorry to be losing Mary as his assistant. She had been encouraging him to look for another for several weeks, yet he had not made any real effort to do so. He harboured the idea that the wedding may yet not happen, with some last-minute chilling of feet by one or other party, and wanted to keep Mary's employment safe for her just in case. It was the Thursday afternoon before the wedding when Moses produced a small parcel wrapped in brown paper and tied with string. He handed it to Mary as they were agreeing to start packing up for the day.

"What is this?" She asked taking the parcel from him with her long slender fingers.

"Just a little something. For your home together."

Mary undid the string and carefully peeled back the paper. Inside was a small rectangular box. She lifted the lid, becoming more curious by the second. A small, wooden tube with a brass ring at each end lay on a piece of dark blue velvet. Mary looked up at Moses with a frown.

"It is a mezuzah. Now I know that neither you nor Philip are Jewish but indulge an old man and allow me to gift this to you both. Inside the tube is a parchment scroll with the first part of the Shema on it. Those are the words that remind us of our responsibilities to God. We hang these, slanted, on our doorposts at about this height." He raised his hand to near his ear.

"In days before, you would see the words themselves written on doorposts and gates. But they drew too much attention, so we have them in these little cases now instead."

Mary nodded, understanding that this was an important symbol of Moses' faith.

"When you hang it up, you must say the blessing,

'Blessed are You, Lord our God, King of the Universe, Who has made us holy with His commandments and commanded us to affix a mezuzah.' And I would be honoured to visit and say it for you."

"Thank you, Moses. As you know, Philip has found a small house for us near to the church. Will you come next week and hang this for us? And you will still come to the wedding on Saturday?"

"I will be there on Saturday, my dear. Sylvia on the hat stall has said she will watch here for a couple of hours."

"Has no one enquired about my job here?"

"Not yet ... a young man, nephew of a man I know at the synagogue might be interested. I will eat with them tomorrow for Shabbat and I shall know more."

Mary sensed that Moses was not being entirely honest with her but did not push him for more details. She knew he lived a quiet life, with no close relatives, and that he had come to care a great deal for her as she had for him.

There were members of the congregation at Saint Agnes who did not approve. This was not a surprise to Philip or the Vicar, and least of all Mary. Some had been openly hostile the whole time Mary had been attending the church. Others only showed their disapproval when the news of the wedding was announced. It took one of the older gentlemen to point out that if the Bishop had given his approval, then that should be good enough for everyone else, for the comments to eventually die down. By the time Philip and Mary walked out of Saint Agnes in the late spring of 1923 as Mr and Mrs Rose, Philip had won almost everyone in the congregation round and cheers and flower petals rained down on the young couple in the sunshine.

Midge's Treasure Hunt

The children sat on the wall next to the Post Office, their sun-tanned legs swinging above the ground. Mark, being the eldest at twelve, was inside the shop buying penny bottles of ginger beer with the coins they had been given for weeding Mrs Smith's vegetable patch that morning. The sun beat down on the dusty road. August 1914 was proving to be a glorious summer, though the thunderstorms that had boiled up regularly in the evenings were making many of the adults grumpy through lack of sleep.

"I'm gasping for a drink!" Hector picked at the dirt under his fingernails.

"I hope it's really gingery, Mother made some last week, but it was just like water." Luke Frampton leaned forward on the wall to see if his brother had made his purchase.

"It wasn't that bad!" Luke's sister Midge elbowed him in the side and almost made him fall off the wall. She was a year older than Luke and two years younger than Mark. Their elder brother Matthew was working on the estate farm, and their youngest brother John was at home at the vicarage with tonsilitis. "I shall miss Mother's cooking when I go away in September."

Jessie frowned at her friend, "Where are you going to?"

"To a new school. Mother and Father think I need to learn how to be a young lady, they say I spend too much time with the boys." Midge's brothers were often called the Gospels around the village of Pangbourne where their father was the vicar. Though there were a few young girls of her age, including Jessie, the Reverend and Mrs Frampton felt their daughter needed some of her rough edges knocking off if she were to get on in life. Mrs Pendersen's School for Girls in Cheltenham had been selected on the basis of a recommendation from one of Georgina Frampton's college friends, and Midge would be boarding there from the following month.

"I shouldn't like to go away from Mother and Father." Jessie said quietly. She was a shy girl, timid and only tagged along with the Framptons because her brother Hector was Luke's best friend.

"It will be an adventure." Midge wasn't at all worried about her impending move.

"I wish we could have an adventure here, I don't want to spend all summer weeding!" Hector was now nibbling on a broken fingernail.

"What adventure?" Mark had appeared with four opened bottles of ginger beer in his arms, which the others took from him. "You girls will have to share one, we didn't have enough for five."

"Hector wants an adventure. I say, we could try and find the Roman treasure." Luke took a mouthful of ginger beer and savoured its tang on his tongue.

"That's an old wives' tale!" Mark chuckled.

"I'm sure it's not! Mr Forbes mentioned it just the other day when I was helping him with his chickens. He said he wished he'd found it so that he wouldn't have to keep working at the boat yard and he could sail away to a tropical island."

"How would we even know where to look?" Jessie handed their bottle back to Midge after taking a sip.

"That's a very good question. There's no map. If there were, the treasure would have been found years ago. We'd have to look for clues." Mark decided not to sit on the wall and risk dropping his bottle.

"If I were a Roman, I would bury my treasure near something that I could recognise when I came back to dig it up again." Luke felt himself to be the authority on the subject, having come top of the class in history again the previous year.

"Are you sure it's on the estate?"

"Everyone says so."

"Why don't we go and take a look when we've finished our drinks?"

"We could make our own map!" Jessie wanted to help her friends and was the most artistic of them all. "I can run home for some paper and a pencil, and I'll meet you at Bees' Corner. Don't leave without me, will you?" She looked worriedly at her older brother.

"Go on then, we'll meet you there in ten minutes." Hector replied, looking meaningfully up at the clock on the church tower across the road.

Ten minutes later the little band were on the path that led from Bee's Corner through the stand of beech trees onto the Basildon Estate. Mark led the way, thrashing at bracken and brambles with a long stick. Luke and Hector were chattering together, pointing out any tree or rock that looked as if it might be from the Roman era. Midge and Jessie brought up the rear, stepping carefully around the brambles that had swung back behind Mark so that their pinafores wouldn't get caught and ripped.

The path opened out onto the grassy expanse below Basildon House. The property was empty; the current owners preferred to spend the summer by the south coast, and all of the tall windows that looked out onto the parkland were covered on the inside with shutters. The estate continued to function in its owners' absence. Matthew Frampton was just one of around twenty men and women whose various occupations helped support the local families and keep Basildon House from falling into ruin. Wheat swayed gold in the distance, almost ready to harvest. Sheep leisurely munched their way across the park, kept away from the formal garden with its fountain by the ha-ha. The heat made everything shimmer.

The children gathered near to the ha-ha and sat in a semi-circle looking outwards across the parkland. The copse on their left from where they had emerged, and the dense woodland to their right framed their view. Beyond the copse, the farmland stretched as far as their eyes could see across the Thames Valley.

"It's so big. Where would we even start?" breathed Jessie, pencil in hand.

"You could start by drawing where the woods are. They've been there forever." Suggested Midge.

After an hour, Jessie had made a good job of drawing each landmark the children thought important, in relation to the house on her sheet of paper (which was the back of an old seed catalogue advertisement poster). Luke and Hector were convinced that the treasure would be buried in the woods, perhaps where two paths crossed. Hector had read a story about pirates recently and was certain treasure was always buried at a cross-roads.

"But Romans weren't pirates you duffer!" Luke laughed and shook his head at his friend.

Midge noticed that Mark was shielding his eyes from the sun and looking intently towards the copse again. "What do you see?"

"The way the ground rises, about twenty feet from the edge of the trees." He pointed. "Like a mound. It looks odd when the rest of the ground is flat and slopes down that way."

The boys grew quiet as they all looked in that direction.

"Should I add it to the map? I don't know how to draw a bump in the ground," Jessie bit the end of her pencil.

"Yes, perhaps draw it as a circle. But I think someone has made it like that. I think if we are going to dig for treasure, that's where we should start."

"Are we really going to dig?" Luke got to his feet with excitement.

"Why not? I suppose if we did find some treasure it would belong to the estate, or perhaps even the King, but we've always been allowed here and I'm sure no one will mind if we did find something."

"You girls better not do any digging. Our mothers would be terribly cross if you went home covered in mud!" Luke put his hands on his hips as he stood over Midge and Jessie.

"What rot! If you're digging, then so are we!" Midge got up and stood nose to nose with her brother.

"Stop it you two! There won't be any mud, the ground is too hard. Midge can dig if she wants. And we'll need someone to make a list of our finds, Jessie can do that. But first we'll need some tools."

Amos Brokenshaw had just poured himself a mug of tea and was about to sit for a few minutes on the old wooden bench in the sun. It was a summer like those of his childhood, and far too hot to be rushing around in the afternoons. He saw the children approaching across the yard and smiled to himself. Always up to something, that lot.

"Af'noon young uns!" He called to them.

"Good afternoon, Amos!" Mark replied. "We'd like to ask you a favour if we may?"

"Ask away, master Frampton. If I can help you with something, then I will."

"Could we borrow some of your tools please? A spade and a fork? And one of those picks to break up the earth?"

"Now then, what would you be wanting tools for?" Amos scratched his ear and swatted away a fly.

"We're digging for treasure!" Luke was too excited to keep it a secret.

"Ahh, well," Amos leaned forward, hands on his knees. "I can see you'd be needing at least a spade then. Got a map, have you?"

"Yes, but it's secret!" Mark said quickly, before Luke had a chance to say where they were hoping to dig. "And we might not find anything. We'd look very silly if we'd told everyone about it and then had nothing to show for our work."

Amos tapped the side of his nose. "Understood. Come with me then young uns, and we'll see what I've got in the shed."

They crossed the cobbled yard and Amos pulled open the door of a large low-roofed building. The smell of creosote, wood shavings and linseed oil was strong in the hot, still afternoon air. Jessie waited outside while the other children followed Amos in. It was as much an Aladdin's cave to the children as any toy shop; tools of every description hung on the walls, stood in rows propped against each other on the floor, and sat on the work bench waiting for repairs. The open door gave some light, but it was still dark in the shed and without Amos to guide them, the children would have tripped over and not known where to look.

Amos let them in so far, then told them to wait while he reached behind a large drum of oil and pulled out a ladies' border spade. He handed it to Mark and said he had a fork to match somewhere. A few moments later, Mark was presented with an equally short fork.

"Now, I shan't let you have a pick, as they can be heavy and dangerous for young uns, but you can have a couple of trowels and forks to go with."

When they rejoined Jessie in the yard, all four children carried something they could dig with.

"Thank you, Amos, these will help us enormously!"

"Yes well, mind you bring them back, don't leave them out overnight in the rain. Shed's open, just stand them inside the door."

"Oh yes, we'll make sure we bring them back. Thank you!" They chorused as they clanged their way back across the yard.

The village children had always had the run of the Basildon House Estate. While they were discouraged from lingering in the formal gardens, the woodland and pastures were available for running, climbing trees and making dens. Few adults paid any attention to these areas, being engaged in their own occupations, and so only the sheep witnessed the little band drag their equipment out across the grass that afternoon. The hillock that was the focus of their search rose gently by almost two feet from the surrounding plane. It was approximately ten feet long and eight feet wide in an oval shape. Had there been games taking place on the parkland, it would have made an excellent place to sit and watch.

Mark suggested they each set out their own space to dig, to avoid any arguments over who eventually found the treasure. They spent another hour scouring the area for stones and branches to edge each of their plots. Mark's, naturally, was in the centre of the top of the mound. Luke and Hector made their plots to the side furthest from Basildon House and the girls marked out a plot on the opposite side and agreed to share it. Jessie was reluctant to do any actual digging and readily handed Midge the small trowel to begin taking up the turf.

The thunderstorms had made the ground softer than it would otherwise have been in the middle of August. The boys made short work of clearing their squares of turf, and by the time the sun dipped below the tops of the trees their holes were around six inches deep. They were all very hungry, and hoped no animals would disturb their efforts during the night as they carried the tools back to Amos' shed.

Amos slept poorly that night. Not only because of the thunder and rain that once again drenched the Thames Valley, but when he did manage to sleep, he dreamed.

Amos had lived all his life on the estate, in the cottage that his parents had been tied to before him. He knew every inch of the grounds and was grateful that the current owners had agreed to him seeing out his days there. In his dream, Amos was young again, no more than ten years old. He was standing by the fountain in the formal garden, watching as a white stallion was led in a circle for some of the adults to admire. As he watched, the stallion reared up and kicked out its forelegs. The adults cowered and the handler worked hard to calm the horse again. Amos had always been wary of horses, but now in his dream he was being told to ride the stallion. He didn't want to; he was scared that the horse would rear again and throw Amos to the ground. Someone was lifting Amos up, pushing him onto the horse's back. There was no saddle, and Amos grasped the silver mane, terrified of letting go. After a few steps he felt the horse tense beneath him and begin to prance sideways. It tossed its head and Amos started to cry. As the horse lifted its front legs again Amos felt himself slipping backwards and he cried out.

Amos woke on the very edge of his narrow bed, arms and legs hanging down outside the thin sheet towards the floor. The faint glow through the open window told him it was almost dawn, and he rolled onto his back for a moment to consider his dream. To his memory, he had never ridden a horse, let alone one so fine as the white stallion he had imagined. Yet it felt familiar to him. Swinging his legs around and placing his feet firmly on the floorboards, Amos got up and went out to the back yard to relieve his bladder. He would take a walk down to the George and Dragon later and see if Bob Beale knew anything about a white horse on the estate.

The children had their chores to do the next morning and had agreed to meet at Bee's Corner after lunch to resume their dig. Hector and Jessie's mother had been cross at the state of Hector's hands and knees when he had arrived home the previous evening, and had used a nail brush to scrub his skin until it glowed red. He could stand the scrubbing on his hands but made up his mind to take an old vest to kneel on instead of the soil the boys were turning over.

Luke woke with a sore throat. John was still confined to bed on the other side of their bedroom and snored loudly as Luke lay staring at the ceiling. He knew John had been unable to eat for a few days and had worried their mother by running a temperature made worse by the heatwave. Luke didn't want to go through the same thing, he liked his food too much to go without. He swallowed a couple of times, and decided a glass of milk would fix things.

By lunchtime, Luke was sweaty and bad tempered. He had been painting the vicarage garden fence and had made regular trips to the water pump to soothe the growing sandpaper sensation in his throat. As he sat at the kitchen table with Mark and Midge, the Frampton's cook bustling around them, Luke struggled with every mouthful of the crusty bread and cheese from his plate. He would not give in; he was not going to let Mark or Hector discover the treasure without him!

"If you children are going to be out all afternoon, you'd best take something to drink with you." Cook said, as if reading Luke's mind. "Little Jenny Day has heat stroke and Mrs Frampton won't want any more of you in bed and ill!"

They were sent out of the kitchen twenty minutes later with Midge carrying a wicker basket containing two stoneware bottles of water partially stoppered with corks, and apples from the garden to see them through until tea.

At Bee's Corner only Hector was there to meet them. Jessie had developed a sore throat overnight and their mother had confined her to the house. Luke looked down at his shoes, not wanting to catch anyone's eye and have them ask if he was feeling alright. He wasn't, he could feel the sweat trickling along his scalp under his blonde hair, but he would die before he owned up to it! Midge could see Luke was sweating and seemed to be wobbling as he walked through the copse. When they reached Amos' shed, Luke picked up the small trowel and fork rather than drag the larger tools to the mound. Midge still had the basket to carry.

That afternoon's digging went at a slower pace than before. The air was sultry, and all of the children were sweating. They stopped to eat the apples at what they thought was about three o'clock. Luke went to sit in the shade of one of the trees at the edge of the copse. After a while he lay down and went to sleep. Mark and the others continued with their digging and while Hector uncovered an old Victorian sixpence and Midge found a broken spoon, the Roman treasure remained elusive.

When they decided to finish for the day, Mark went to wake Luke up. With a great effort Luke got to his feet and Mark was worried that he might have to carry his little brother home. Luke was clearly unwell, and his voice was husky when he tried to speak. His throat felt like broken glass every time he swallowed, but he was grateful that they had saved some of the water for him to drink before they set off. When Amos saw Luke he told the boy to sit on the bench. The others put the tools away while Amos brought his wheelbarrow into the yard. Luke was instructed to sit in it and Amos wheeled him home with the three children marching along in front of him. Mrs Frampton was cross and concerned in equal measure and thanked Amos profusely before sending Hector on home and her children up to their bedrooms.

Amos pushed his now empty wheelbarrow back to his cottage, thinking of the conversation he had had with Bob Beale. There had been a white stallion at the estate, though before Amos and

Bob's time. Bob remembered a story told by his father about the then owner who had been given a white stallion for his twenty fifth birthday. It had been a spirited animal, well matched with its new owner, and the pair had forged a strong bond. Amos knew how animals could befriend humans. He'd had several dogs during his sixty-three years, but never a horse.

There was no storm that night. Thunder rumbled around the Thames Valley all the next morning and just as Mark and Midge were called to the kitchen for their lunch, it began to rain. There would be no digging that afternoon, but, Mark whispered, it would keep the ground soft. They had to wait for the following afternoon before they could continue their labours. By then Hector had also been struck down with a sore throat, so Midge was able to wield the ladies' spade while Mark broke the ground with the fork. Then they swapped tools, and cleared and loosened their plots until Midge spotted something in her pit. It was almost two feet down and she picked up the small trowel to work away some more of the dirt around the object.

Mark looked across at his sister. "Have you found something?"

"I'm not sure. I don't think it is treasure. It's the wrong colour."

"Let me see." Mark climbed out of his hole and knelt at the edge of Midge's. They both looked down at the grey object that stood a little proud from the ground that Midge had carefully cleared around it.

"It looks... like bone."

The children looked at each other with worried faces.

"Should we cover it back up?" Midge asked.

Mark sat back on his heels. "I rather think we should tell Constable Armstrong. Come on, let's take the tools back to Amos."

"Do you think it's a person buried there? I don't want it to be a person, Mark," Midge's lip began to tremble.

Mark put his arm around his little sister. He didn't want it to be a person either, unless it was a Roman soldier of course.

"Finished already?" Amos was sipping his tea on the bench when the children returned.

"Yes, we... we feel a bit tired today." Mark didn't want to tell anyone what they had found until Constable Armstrong had been informed. He had a feeling that the adults would take over their dig as soon as they knew, and if it was a Roman soldier, then Mark would be told to keep away.

"That tonsilitis is running amok through the village. We'll all have it before the month's out I expect. Find any more bits of treasure, missy?"

Midge looked at Mark and shook her head.

Constable Armstrong was in the little police house, leaning his elbows on the table in the room that served as a reception, reading a newspaper. He enjoyed his job in the quiet village of Pangbourne. He knew everyone and everyone knew him. Very rarely was any crime committed, and even then, it was usually interlopers from the larger town of Reading some ten miles east along the river Thames. He felt the lack of crime was due to his visible presence and made sure to take his bicycle out at least once a day around the lanes and up to the cottage hospital for a cup of tea and a chat with the Matron.

He heard the children talking outside before they came into the police house through the front door that he kept open when he was at home.

"Let me do the talking, Midge."

"But I found it!"

"Yes, but we don't know what it really is. And I'll need to explain everything carefully."

Midge scowled, feeling much braver now that there was some distance between her and the treasure pit she had dug. She nodded her head and they went inside. It took a moment for their eyes to adjust from the brilliance of the sunshine to the darker interior.

Constable Armstrong was smiling as he usually did. "Hullo, you two."

"Hello Constable Armstrong," Mark didn't feel half as grown up as he was trying to be. "We would like to report some treasure, sir. Except it's not really treasure..."

"Treasure, eh?" These long summer holidays often brought out the children's imaginations and Constable Armstrong was happy to play along.

"Yes, well no. You see we've been digging for treasure ..."

"I found it!" Midge couldn't stop herself.

"Midge, I said I would explain!"

"Alright, why don't you sit down on the bench there and I'll make some notes in my pocketbook. You can tell me all about it, Midge."

The little girl swelled with pleasure at being listened to. So often she felt invisible amongst her brothers. She and Mark sat on the bench and Constable Armstrong came around to sit on the edge of his desk, notebook and pencil in hand.

"Let's start at the beginning, shall we? Where is it you've been digging?"

Between them, Midge and Mark recounted their explorations. Despite their jumbled narration, Constable Armstrong frowned when he learned they had been digging on the estate, and his frown deepened when Midge finally announced "It looks like a bone!"

It was as Mark had feared. He tried to explain that he was interested in seeing if it really was a Roman soldier buried under the mound but Constable Armstrong was clear: the children must stay away from the site until a thorough investigation had been carried out. When Mark and Midge had left the police house, on the strict instruction to go straight home, Constable Armstrong set the wheels of detection in motion. He telephoned his superiors in Reading and explained he would be assembling a small digging party from the estate workers, and could Reading send a Sergeant down just in case. He was told one would be arriving by train the following morning but was given the go ahead to begin further excavations.

As the thunder once again rumbled around the Thames Valley, four men stood with their shirt sleeves rolled up, looking into a shallow trench.

"I don't think we need to clear any more, lads." Constable Armstrong said as he leaned on his spade.

"I told you it was too long to be a human bone. Didn't I tell him, Fred?"

"You did Amos, you did. Still, better to be sure." Fred took out his handkerchief and mopped his face and neck.

"You got enough to write a report or whatever it is you do, have you?" Amos looked at Constable Armstrong.

"Yes. Let's fill it in before the rain starts again."

It was a week later when the children were finally allowed back to the estate. Midge had been the next to be struck down with tonsilitis, though she recovered far quicker than her brothers had done. Hector had visibly lost some of his chubbiness during his sickness, and Jessie looked gaunt despite her suntanned face, arms and legs. Mark led the little group back again through the copse and into the yard where Amos greeted them cheerfully.

"How do, young uns!"

"Good morning, Amos. We came to say sorry for causing a disturbance for you. Mother says we should have asked permission before we started digging." Luke was still much aggrieved that he had missed out on finding anything.

"No harm done, master Frampton."

"Did you see, there was a report about it in the newspaper?" Mark held a copy out for Amos to take.

"I'm famous." Beamed Midge.

"No you're not, silly, it's not even on the front page." Hector replied.

Amos unfolded the newspaper and opened it to the third page where local news stories and events appeared. He had seen it a few days before, but understood the children hoped to be the first to tell him of it. He cleared his throat theatrically and read aloud.

"Children Uncover Bones. On Thursday last, a group of local children who were playing on the Basildon House Estate unearthed what at first appeared to be the remains of a body. Margaret Frampton, aged ten, raised the alarm when a shard of femur emerged from the soil she had been removing. On further investigation, the local police constable confirmed that the bones were that of a horse and no further action was needed, save to replace the soil and reseed the area."

"I'd still like to find the Roman treasure," Luke said wistfully.

Amos refolded the newspaper and gave it back to Mark. "I think," he said, "you've got all the treasure you need right here."

THE SWIMMING GALA

In the early 1900s, a fitness craze swept Britain. School children were marshalled into outdoor squares and encouraged (sternly) to move together in regimented synchronised programmes of exercise. Competitions were arranged between rival schools and exhibitions displayed at festivals and holidays. In spa towns, where bathing in the waters had been long encouraged, this fitness obsession also manifested in swimming galas for girls and boys.

Cheltenham had three swimming baths open to the public and used at various times by the local schools. The largest and most elegantly designed was the Montpellier baths which had been in situ at the end of Oriel Road for one hundred years. Not only was it a public bath house which included a pool of twenty feet by ten feet, it also had various steam rooms, and an operation for crystalising the salt from the spa waters which was sold around the country as *The Real Cheltenham Salts*. A bakery, which made use of the energy that was produced in the salt-making process, had been opened for a short while on the site, until space was needed for more showers and treatment rooms, as well as a smaller pool which was reserved for ladies. Indeed, the Montpellier baths were a real attraction for the better class of patron, which included the Duke of Wellington who attended daily during a two-week stay in the town.

Eleven-year-old Caroline Munhead stared at the tattered cotton bathing costume in her hands with horror. "Oh no!" she breathed.

"What's up?" asked Midge to her left who was pulling her towel out of her cloth bag.

"Look! I can't wear this; someone has cut it all up and made huge holes in it!" Caroline held up the garment in front of her. The once neatly stitched navy-blue and white ensemble now resembled an offering for the rag and bone man.

Helen looked up from tying her canvas shoes. "Gracious! You must have some enormous moths at home!"

"It's no joke Helen, someone has done this deliberately, see how the edges are cut cleanly?" Midge was inspecting the cloth. "When did you last wear it?"

"Last Friday. It was perfectly alright when I packed it on Monday morning. And I'm sure it was alright when I put it into my bag this morning." Caroline felt tears welling in her eyes. She was due at the poolside for the Young Ladies Two Lengths Front Crawl in ten minutes, and she couldn't possibly wear her bathing suit now.

"So it must have happened earlier today, while we've been watching the boys races." Midge said quietly. She looked around the Ladies changing room and her gaze rested on the small knot of girls in the far corner who were huddled together and giggling.

"Well, look sharp," said Helen, "someone must have a spare you can borrow." She raised her voice so that their classmates could hear above the general chatter of six schools' swimming teams, "do any of you from Mrs Pendersen's have a spare costume?"

Caroline was now turning her cloth bag inside out. "My cap is missing too! Someone has stolen my bathing cap!" She felt a mixture of embarrassment and real dismay. Caroline loved swimming; it gave her a sense of freedom and elegance that she rarely felt on dry land with her above-average height and big feet. Not only did she enjoy swimming, she was also rather good at it, and had been first choice for the race out of Mrs Pendersen's older girls.

Two of the other girls in Mrs Pendersen's team had spare costumes but both girls were only just over five feet tall. Caroline was already a good five inches taller, and their costumes did not fit however hard Midge and Helen tugged and pulled at them. Caroline eventually told them to stop for fear of being cut in half herself.

"I'll just have to withdraw from the race," she said dejectedly as she started to pull her vest back over her head.

"But you're the favourite, you can't pull out. There must be something we can do." Midge sat next to her friend and would have put her arm around Caroline's shoulders had she not also only been four feet ten inches tall.

The other girls were now leaving the changing rooms to take up their positions on the wooden seating around the pool. The huddle of girls from the Fortescue School had now formed a line and were filing past Caroline and her friends. Ethel Corsham, the true favourite for the race Caroline was entered in, sneered as she approached Caroline.

"Oh dear, has something happened to your bathing suit?"

"It's ruined ..." Caroline began.

"Just a tiny mishap, nothing to be worried about. Run along, there's a dear, your friends will be waiting for you." Chipped in Helen, getting to her feet. The tallest of the three friends, she stood eye to eye with Ethel.

Mrs Pendersen appeared in the doorway, looking for her team of young swimmers. She had high hopes this year of a clean sweep of firsts, which would mean winning the Ladies Trophy. They had lost out by only three points to the Ladies College the year before. Mrs Pendersen did not hold with the notion that competition was bad for young girls. When the Fortescue School team had filed past her, she strode over to where her team were looking disheartened.

"Come along now girls, the first race is due to start shortly. We have every chance of winning the Ladies Trophy this year, but only if you are all in your places when the referee blows his whistle to start the afternoon session. Caroline, why have you not changed?"

Once again, Caroline held up her bathing costume displaying its numerous holes. "I don't have my cap either, Mrs Pendersen."

"How on earth...?" Mrs Pendersen brought her had up to her temple in amazement.

"I'll bet it was the Fortescue girls." Midge proclaimed.

"Oh Midge, we can't prove they did it." Caroline couldn't stop the tears now as she realised she would be the cause of the school not winning the trophy after all.

"That's quite enough, Margaret. Caroline, put your gymslip back on and everyone out now to the benches. Leave this to me." She turned on her heel and left the girls to finish getting ready.

"She looked like thunder!" Midge whispered to Caroline once their teacher was safely out of earshot.

"I'm not surprised. I feel awful, Midge, I've let everyone down."

"Don't be a donkey, of course you haven't. Someone is trying to cheat, and nothing good will come of it." Midge sounded much older than her eleven years and four months.

Mrs Pendersen's team were the last to take their places on the wooden benches to one side of the pool. As they sat down, they could see Mrs Pendersen was in heated, animated conversation with Miss Scotley, the gym mistress of the Fortescue School. The girls from that team were still giggling to each other until a stern look from Miss Scotley silenced them.

The referee was about to blow his whistle when Mrs Pendersen and Miss Scotley approached him. Another short exchange of words was had, inaudible above the murmurings of the spectators, then the referee nodded. He blew his whistle and beckoned to the first swimmers to approach the end of the pool, while Mrs Pendersen and Miss Scotley made their way to where Caroline sat at the end of a bench. She was feeling wretched; people were looking at her and pointing, and she knew it was because she was not in a bathing suit like the other girls. Her cheeks were glowing red.

"Caroline, we have a solution. Come with us quickly." Mrs Pendersen gestured towards the changing rooms.

Once inside, away from questioning stares and able to hear each other speak, Miss Scotley explained that she had brought her own bathing suit and as she was only slightly taller than Caroline, it might fit. As the cheers of the crowd grew for the first race, the women helped Caroline quickly undress and pull on the knickerbockers. They came up to Caroline's armpits, but at least they weren't too small. Next she pulled on the top, which fitted her a little better. Miss Scotley put a sash around Caroline's waist and tied it as tightly as she dared, in the hope that the knickers would not fall down as Caroline swam.

"Thank you, Miss Scotley. Hurry now Caroline, retake your place ready for your race to be called." Mrs Pendersen handed Caroline Miss Scotley's bathing cap and propelled her out of the changing room.

A few minutes later, Caroline stood on the pool edge, Ethel Corsham to her left and a very small girl from the Ladies College on her right. Ethel was no longer giggling. She had scowled at Caroline as they lined up to take their positions, and Caroline could see the frowns on the faces of Ethel's team-mates. Caroline tried to ignore Ethel and focus on the race. She knew Ethel was the favourite, but Caroline's technique had improved over the previous year, and she was a strong swimmer. She had a chance if she could get a good start.

"Take your marks!" barked the referee.

The girls crouched.

"You're going to lose." Muttered Ethel just loud enough for Caroline to hear.

The whistle blew.

Caroline couldn't hear the cheers from the spectators or her school friends as the water rushed over her head and she began to swim in long confident strokes. The lanes in the pool were narrow and Caroline was conscious that she had left the swimmer from the Ladies College behind as she approached the tiled wall at the far end. Ethel was almost level with Caroline; she had had to expend more energy than she had expected just to keep up with Caroline and her lungs were beginning to burn.

As the two girls reached the wall, Caroline was slightly ahead. She turned and started off on the second length when she felt a hand grip her leg. Ethel had dived lower in the water on her turn and had grabbed at Caroline to put her off her stroke. It almost worked. In a second Caroline realised what was happening and she kicked for all her worth to shake off her rival.

The spectators nearest the pool were pointing at the water. They saw what Ethel had done and were shouting and waving at the referee who stood waiting at the other end ready to declare the winner. Some of the older boys got to their feet and waved their caps to get the referee's attention.

Caroline knew none of this. She kicked and crawled through the water, stretching her arms as far as they would reach and pulling them back again with all her might. She dared not breathe; she wanted nothing to slow her down. She hadn't even been counting her strokes and the shock as her arm crashed into the edge of the pool made her gulp for air and swallow a good deal of water. She was coughing and gasping and didn't notice the referee come to stand by Ethel's lane with his arm raised. Ethel had won by a fingertip.

The pool erupted in boos and jeers and shouts of 'Cheat!' and 'She was robbed!'. Two of the older boys raced around the edge of the pool and protested loudly to the referee. He held up his hand to try and calm the noise so that he could hear. One of the school masters followed his pupils around the side of the pool, and remonstrated with the referee, explaining that he and many others had witnessed the winner interfering with the other girl at the turn. Another school master joined them, eager to confirm what he had seen. The weight of observed evidence was overwhelming.

The referee nodded his head and indicated that the men and boys should return to their seats. Then he returned to the head of Ethel's lane. The girls were still catching their breath in the water and looked up at him in anticipation. The referee lifted his arms and made the shape of a cross, indicating that Ethel had been disqualified. Then he stepped across to Caroline's lane and lifted one arm into the air, blowing his whistle at the same time. Caroline had won her race.

There was little time for Caroline to bask in the glory of her win. She climbed out of the pool after the girl from the Ladies College, grabbed her towel and followed the other swimmers into the changing room. Looking back, she could see Ethel in tears and being consoled unconvincingly by Miss Scotley. The gym mistress was guiding Ethel by the shoulders towards her towel and trying not to get herself wet in the process. Shivering, Caroline hurried to get out of her borrowed costume as the next race began.

That night in the bedroom Caroline, Midge and Helen shared with two other girls, Caroline sat in her nightdress on her bed and held the golden pin with its bright blue ribbon in her hand. She had never won anything before, and she was so eager to write and tell her older brother Freddie all about it. Freddie was an excellent sportsman; he would appreciate her achievement.

"You'll wear it out if you keep stroking it." Helen muttered from beneath her covers.

Midge was already asleep and gently snoring in her bed. Caroline carefully put the pin on the little table between hers and Helen's beds and climbed under her own sheet and blankets. She lay on her side and looked at Helen.

"We won the trophy."

"No thanks to Ethel." Helen said sleepily. "You did very well." That praise was worth as much to Caroline as any prize.

THE BRIGHT YOUNG THINGS

THE EVENING BREEZE THROUGH the open window was warm, humid, damp. The rain earlier that day had been welcome at the time but now its evaporation heralded an uncomfortable night. Helen sat at her dressing table and stared at herself in the tall mirror. She pushed her shoulders back, pouted her lips a little, narrowed her eyes, then relaxed again. It was a routine she had performed many times, and always just before a party or social event of some kind.

It was not really her dressing table, any more than it was really her bedroom. Just another in a series of temporary accommodations she had made use of. Moderately wealthy and connected parents were useful, as were their friends and more distant relatives. Tonight, she was in London; tomorrow she would return to Devon, to her real home, and then onwards after a few days to wherever the next invitation took her. She had made her own connections also. Four years at Mrs Pendersen's School for Girls in Cheltenham had been worth it for those alone. The following summer in Italy had been another form of instruction, Bianca had seen to that. Helen smiled at the memory of long hot days in the fields outside Naples and the smell of lavender in Bianca's long black hair.

She picked up her brush and stroked her own sleek, short dark hair a few times before placing the brush back down on the dressing table. Her reflection gazed back with its green eyes and yet-to-be-made-up face. What is the point of all this, her reflection asked. All this endless roaming from party to party, what are we trying to achieve here? What are we trying to prove?

It was not marriage; Helen knew that for sure. Of course, lesbians did marry, many of them, it would seem from the gossip and observations Helen had gathered. But it was not an outcome she was interested in pursuing. The very thought of some man's hands on her body for anything other than a dance or two made her stomach churn. Any more than two dances almost inevitably led to the man presuming an open invitation, in her experience. Was that why she had taken to endlessly moving from one party to the next – to try and outrun those who would try to become too familiar? Perhaps, she conceded.

Helen stood and picked up her dress from the bed. She lifted it over her head and let it cascade down over her slender figure. The pale blue chiffon encrusted with silver beads ended just above her knees. Her stockings were sheer and sparkled slightly as she crossed the room and slipped on her cream leather shoes. After fastening the buckles, she stood up, now almost five feet ten in height. She glanced out of the window towards the dome of Saint Paul's in the distance. Perhaps one day she might see inside the cathedral. Perhaps she should make more effort to take in her surroundings, the history, the architecture. But it did always seem an effort after such late nights.

Tommy's stomach growled as he walked along Kensington High Street. He turned heads as he passed by the men leaving their places of employment and women hurrying home with their shopping. Not for Tommy the sober brown and black suits and bowler hats or flap caps worn by almost all of his fellow Londoners. Tommy strode along in a blue suit in a dogtooth check fabric, his royal blue waistcoat with brass buttons – grown slightly less snug-fitting over the recent months – visible as his hands held the small change and handkerchief in his trouser pockets. He had slicked back his hair, which was in need of a trim. There was too much month left at the end of his money however, and a trip to the barber would have to wait if he were not to die of starvation in the meantime.

Tommy stepped into the Cobourg House café and took a seat at a table in the window. The waitress arrived promptly and took his order for coffee, corned beef hash and fried eggs. It would leave him just enough for a packet of cigarettes and a drink at the club that evening. Three days until his allowance was due again, and he would have to avoid Mrs Proctor and her passive aggressive request for rent in advance for the rest of the week. He was fairly confident she wouldn't put his belongings out on the street, as he did always pay up in the end.

While he waited for his food, Tommy lit the last cigarette in his case and watched the Kensington populace going about their business in the early evening drizzle. He noticed a young man loitering outside the public conveniences, obviously to Tommy much younger than he was trying to appear. Most of the pedestrians ignored him. Then one older man approached, catching the younger man's attention. A few words briefly exchanged before the pair descended the steps into the toilets below. Tommy sighed. His food arrived, and he took a sip of his coffee, still watching the conveniences across the street. He could easily picture the scene below street level, the cramped confines of the stall, the cold surface of the tiles, the stench of men. He knew it well, to his enduring shame.

His early days in London had almost been his last. Arriving with a rudimentary understanding of society and a few pounds in his pocket, determined to prove to his father that he could make something of himself away from the factory, he had been easy prey. Tommy was open, generous and far too trusting and naïve. His preference for male company shone like a beacon to those who saw no problem in using him to their advantage or for their entertainment. There had been difficult lessons to learn, the hardest being humility when two strong hands had pulled him up out of a pile of rubbish in an alley behind the Turk's Head pub in Whitechapel early one morning, his trousers around his ankles and a brass band playing in his head.

The old Belgian man had waited while Tommy adjusted his clothing, vomited, and then unsteadily shuffled along to the end of the alley. They had walked in silence to the older man's house, and over the following three days and nights, Tommy had recovered enough of his self-respect to start out again. He still lived precariously, but no longer relied on evening drinking pals to provide a bed for the night. The Belgian was a refugee, keen to be kind to his fellow Londoners now that he felt safe enough to do so. Two trusting immigrants together, they were both grateful for the other's platonic company and Tommy stayed in the spare room for almost four months.

Tommy was looking forward to that evening. He was starting to make some less rakish friends in the city and had managed to get himself nominated and seconded to join the Canterbury Club. There was to be a party that night, one of the few occasions the Club would permit women entry, to celebrate the birthday of one of the senior members. It would be a chance to meet a better class of people and perhaps lead to some opportunity for employment. He needed to find a job where he could be creative without being regimented. How lucky he had been to miss out on the War – Tommy would never have survived the army regime, he thought as he tucked into his dinner. Boarding school was meant to prepare children for that kind of existence, but his time at Salcombe College had been more of a pastoral instruction. The Brothers had been strict, but the curriculum was more related to the existence and sustenance of the College.

Helen arrived at the Canterbury Club with her great aunt Felicity at a quarter past nine. Their driver would return for them at one the next morning, though Helen often declined the ride and followed the crowd to whichever establishment they moved on to where alcohol, cocaine and music were still available. As they handed over their coats and moved into the main reception room, Helen's heart sank. It was, as she had feared, a party for older people. Her great aunt was already greeting friends and acquaintances, and Helen glided along beside her dutifully while appraising the other guests. A couple of women closer to her age stood together sipping cocktails. A short young man with spectacles and very short-cropped hair hovered by the fireplace looking as if he needed a drink but couldn't reach the waiter's tray.

"And this is my great niece, Helen Postgate," Felicity was introducing her to a group of white-haired ancients who reeked of perfume and cigars, all leaning forwards to better hear the conversation.

Helen smiled sweetly, taking in each of their names in turn and agreeing that it was such a splendid party. Four hours of this would be the death of her, she sighed inwardly.

There was a crash across the room and a shriek of a woman. Everyone turned towards the commotion. Helen was fortunate that she did not need to stand on tip-toe to see what was going on. The shrieking woman was now fanning herself furiously while her male associate was gently dabbing at her frock with his handkerchief and scowling at a much younger man in a blue suit. The young man was clearly trying not to laugh while offering the woman another glass of champaign and edging away from the couple. On the floor was a tray and a litter of broken glass and champaign, and in his attempt to move away, the young man backed into the approaching stewards arriving on the scene with a mop and dustpan and brush. The bump from behind sent the young man forwards again, resulting in more alcohol pouring onto the woman's dress, more shrieks, and the older man furiously pushing the younger away.

As Felicity and her friends muttered amongst themselves as to the kind of young person allowed into the Club, Helen weaved her way across the room and claimed the space between the older and younger man, carefully avoiding the broken glass.

"Good evening, Major Collins! And Mrs Collins, how lovely to see you again, I believe the ladies' withdrawing room is to the left over there. I'm sure the stewards would bring you a clean damp cloth." The final sentence was spoken to the nearest steward, accompanied by a raised eyebrow. The steward nodded and indicated to Mrs Collins which way she should go. Helen turned to the younger man who was still chuckling to himself as he brushed spills of champaign from his suit.

"And you, sir, should probably escort me to the terrace!"

Tommy looked up at the girl standing before him. She had spoken with the confidence of someone twice her age, and he was surprised to see she could be no more than eighteen. She tilted her head, waiting for him to reply.

"I'm afraid you will have to lead the way, I'm not hugely familiar with this place just yet."

"And quite possibly you won't have a chance to become so, if you carry on like that. Come along." Helen turned and walked through the crowd that parted dutifully as she approached.

The terrace led out to a small garden with a view across the Thames. Lamps had been lit to illuminate the pathway around the garden, and at intervals along the stone wall that separated it from the flagstones of the terrace itself. Two sets of French windows cast further light onto the puddled surface, and Helen instinctively moved out of the doorway and across to the wall. Tommy trotted behind, intrigued and relieved to have been rescued from his unfortunate clumsiness.

"Do tell me you have a cigarette!" Helen gasped.

"Of course," Tommy opened his case and took out two, then fumbled for his matches. Helen produced a lighter from her beaded purse and handed it to Tommy.

"Here. Matches get so damp. I've not seen you before, who are you?"

"Thanks. No, well, I've only been here a couple of times before and then I was accepted last week. I never even knew this terrace was here. Tommy Gersen-Fisch at your service." He held out his hand which Helen shook firmly.

"Helen Postgate. My great aunt is friends with the Club Secretary, Michael Cobbes MBE. It is one of the most boring places in London, why on earth would you want to become a member?"

"My father thought I should join. Persuaded one of his friend's sons to nominate me, and a pal of his to second. Father thinks it will give me connections." Tommy looked out over the garden towards the river and heard the youth in his own voice.

"If you want to become a banker, then I suppose it will. But you don't appear to be someone who would want to be a banker."

"I don't. Not a businessman at all really. To tell you the truth I have no real plans to become anything. I'm only in London because it's not Sheffield. Father didn't want me hanging around any more than I wanted to stay, so I came to see if the streets really were paved with gold."

"And you found...?"

"I found they are covered with the same horse shit as everywhere else. There is a charm about the old place though, don't you think?"

"London? Oh yes. But you need to know the right people."

"Do you? Know the right people, I mean." Tommy could not disguise the hope in his voice.

Helen drew deeply on her cigarette and studied the young man before her. He was so obviously out of his depth at the Club, but there was something about him. Something that made her think he would be jolly good fun to know. Great aunt Felicity would be perfectly safe here with her friends, and as long as Helen returned before one o'clock she wouldn't have to find a taxi by herself.

"I do, but you won't find them here tonight. Have you been to the Black Cat? Or to Albertine's?"

Tommy shook his head.

"Then you haven't lived, darling. Let's have one more drink here, and then I will take you to meet some people more of our sort."

Helen woke, stiff and with one hand numb and heavy. The room was dark, but she could make out a large clock on the wall and the hands seemed to say twenty minutes to five. She moved her numb arm to hang by her side for a moment encouraging the blood to flow and surveyed the various bodies around the room as the inevitable pins and needles began. Some were on the floor, entwined. Some sprawled or curled in chairs as she was. Some covered with coats or blankets, some in states of undress. Someone was snoring quietly on the other side of the room. Counting the bodies she could see, Helen guessed around half the party had made their way upstairs or on to another location. Where had she kicked off her shoes? Where was Tommy?

She gingerly sat upright, wriggling her fingers. One of her shoes was visible underneath the cocktail trolley and she hoped the other would be nearby. A recollection of dancing barefoot with a woman with flame red hair came to her. She would never find her stockings without putting the room light on, but thankfully she could feel she had been sitting, and sleeping, on her own beaded purse. Helen got up and quietly began to step over the debris of the night before.

Tommy sat at the bottom of the staircase and looked again at his watch. He didn't feel he could leave without making sure Helen was alright. He knew she wasn't in any of the bedrooms, as he had checked cautiously after leaving the one he and Lars had stumbled into around midnight. Helen had been right, she did know their sort of people. He had no idea how Helen could have guessed that he was attracted to other men, but she was clearly attracted to other women, of that he was now in no doubt. Was that why he felt the need to wait for her now?

The door handle opposite Tommy's perch turned slowly and with a click the door opened, revealing Helen. She was clutching her coat, bag and shoes, barefoot with mascara circles under her eyes and only a faint trace of lipstick. Seeing Tommy, she smiled and nodded her head silently towards the front door.

Outside in the street, they took their bearings from the sign on the railings that surrounded the square of lawn and flower beds. Warwick Square, Helen had a vague notion, was in Pimlico and she would need to head south and across the river to great aunt Felicity's house in Vauxhall.

"Which way do you need to go?" She asked as they reached the entrance to the square.

"Towards Kensington, I shall attempt to find Chelsea and then I'll know my way. But look here, you can't walk all the way to Vauxhall at this hour!"

"I shall have to find a cab. I wonder if there are any coffee houses open, I'm jolly hungry."

They looked up and down the street.

"Bound to be somewhere open around Victoria. We could walk that way." Tommy offered Helen his arm.

They walked slowly in the hour before dawn, skirting around puddles and crossing almost deserted residential streets with the first lights appearing at windows on top floors and in basements. They talked about the night before, affirming each other's understanding of their attractions and feeling a sense of camaraderie. Over coffee and pastries when they finally found a café, they continued their inquiries of each other until, sated and sleepy, Helen leaned back in her chair.

"So, what you are telling me, is that I shall be paying for our breakfast, and then you will hail me a cab and send me on my way back to Vauxhall?"

Tommy lit the last cigarette in his case and handed it to Helen. "I'm afraid so old thing. No cash until the first of the month. At least I can eat at the Canterbury and put it on my tab, and who knows one might bump into Lars again."

"I shall be on the twelve fifteen train back to Plymouth later, otherwise I would suggest meeting tonight for dinner somewhere. I'll be back in London at the end of next month though, it's my cousin Gordon's birthday and he is hiring a boat for a party on the river. I shall leave a message for you at the Canterbury. It will be nice to have a pal to go about with. One gets a little tired of always being seen with ancient relatives."

L'Hotel Le Negresco, La Promenade des Anglais

Platform one at the Gard du Nice was obscured by the steam that swirled from the stationary train. Doors slammed, men shouted for porters and errand boys to help with luggage, women chattered quietly in French, English, Italian and German. There was very little room on the platform; those boarding the train jostled with those trying to leave it, the evening sunset blinding those who could see through the steam. A child began to wail, until she was swept up into her mother's arms and carried inside the waiting carriage.

It got busier each year, Monsieur Abenard thought to himself as he glanced out of the ticket office window at the platform. He could remember when the summers in Nice were peaceful, without these incomers disturbing the town and demanding rooms, food, drink and entertainment. The refugees of the previous decade had made way for the new rich travellers, and Monsieur did not think he liked it. Madame Abenard had relatives inland at Castellane; they had often talked of moving there to be nearer Madame's nieces and nephews, and the idea was certainly growing in attraction to Monsieur Abenard.

A German couple approached Monsieur Abenard's ticket window asking in halting French for passage to Paris. As Monsieur Abenard tried to explain the train connections to the couple in his own rough German, he did not see the events unfolding on Platform one.

"You there! Yes, you, Porter! We are in need of assistance." Great Aunt Agnes Fellows had a surprisingly loud and commanding voice for a woman so small of stature. She had spotted a man with a luggage trolley through the steam and was waving to attract his attention. Florence, her great niece, was occupied in stacking their smaller cases and bags on the platform as a Wagon Lit attendant brought them from the baggage compartment. As Florence stepped backwards and turned towards her great aunt, the older lady also made to turn. Suddenly through the steam a young man ploughed into both ladies, sending them and several of their bags sprawling.

The quick-thinking porter managed to catch Great Aunt Agnes before she hit the stone platform. Florence toppled over the stack of cases and landed with a thump on her side, her hat flying off and her skirts riding up to expose her stockings and slim legs. The young man, dressed in a striped blazer and grey flannels also lost his hat, a straw boater, which wheeled along the platform and dropped neatly down onto the tracks below. Willie Clyde Martin Jnr swore as he felt his knee graze on the hard surface of the flagstones. Then he realised he had partially landed on a young woman and the contents of at least one of her bags and his own were now strewn together between them.

"Monsieur! Est-ce que tu vas bien?" The porter asked over Great Aunt Agnes' shoulder.

Willie looked back the way he had just come. The men had stopped some yards away and were talking together. He watched them glance at him before they hurried away and out of the station.

"Monsieur?"

"I say, could someone help me please?" Florence had rolled onto her knees and was scrabbling about trying to retrieve her great aunt's belongings.

Willie pulled himself together. "I am fine," and turning to Florence, "I am so very sorry, please forgive my clumsiness ma'am, this steam, hard to see clearly. Here, let me..." He reached out to take hold of a spectacles case at the same moment Florence's had grasped it. "I think that's mine." He said, his hand over Florence's.

"I don't think so, my great aunt has had this case for some time now. Perhaps that one is yours?" She gestured to another spectacles case a few feet away.

Willie hesitated. They both looked very similar. "Well, yes, I think you're right. I'm sure had I been wearing mine I might not have tumbled into you." He smiled at the pretty young woman dressed in pale blue beside him.

"Do hurry yourself, Florence. The porter is waiting." Great Aunt Agnes could see the way Willie was looking at her great niece and was not about to encourage a suitor in the middle of a railway station.

After several more minutes of retrieving their belongings, Willie and Florence followed Great Aunt Agnes and the porter through the station concourse and out to the street. Loudly in English, Great Aunt Agnes instructed the porter to obtain them a taxi to the Hotel le Negresco.

"I say, that's where I'm staying. What a stroke of luck! Would you mind if I share your ride?"

Great Aunt Agnes looked down her nose at the young man. "I hardly think..."

Florence interjected, "Of course you must; we don't mind at all, do we, Great Aunt?"

A taxi pulled up, acknowledging the porter's wave. Willie began to help put the cases onto the roof of the vehicle and Great Aunt Agnes reluctantly agreed that he could travel with them. She was tired and in poor spirits after days of rail and boat accommodation, despite the service being excellent on the Blue Train. She was not getting any younger, and the journey felt longer each time she made it. She had thought Florence should be introduced to the Riviera society now that she was approaching the end of her time at the finishing school, but a random stranger was not Great Aunt Agnes' idea of a suitable match. She had hoped to find a young European Duke or Count for her great niece, a man with prospects and breeding. This American dandy did not fit into her plan at all.

Florence had been excited about the trip. She had written to her neighbour Caroline back in Cheltenham as soon as her great aunt had invited her, about how she hoped to have cocktails with a film star and see the very latest fashions on display along the promenade. Hadn't Charlie Chaplin taken the Blue Train recently? She was sure she had read about it in the newspaper.

Florence was well aware that her family were considerably less affluent than her school fellows. Her parents were both teachers, not bankers or property tycoons or Maharajahs, and her great aunt having married well, was now funding her education as well as subsidising her parent's rent. Florence's brother Timothy had secured an apprenticeship as a shipping clerk at Gloucester docks and was expected to rise through the company on his own merits. What merits did Florence have? Very few, as far as her great aunt was concerned, beyond the deportment and language skills expected of a young woman in society. Florence considered her looks to be her greatest asset and knew she turned heads when in company.

As Willie got into the taxi he looked once more to see if he could spot his pursuers. Their long coats were conspicuous in the warm late spring weather, but they had melted away. He let out a sigh of relief and considered his situation. He was meant to be in Italy by now. He wondered if his contact there would wait for him; surely the information and items Willie was carrying would be reason to wait. He hoped so. If only he hadn't got quite so drunk in Paris, and hadn't talked quite so loudly, things might not have got quite so out of hand. And yet, for all his poor luck, here he was in the company of a rather beautiful young woman who happened to be staying at the same hotel he had booked into two days before. Life wasn't all bad, Willie decided.

Great Aunt Agnes had taken a small suite on the second floor, overlooking the Promenade and the glittering sea beyond. Florence had an adjoining room, which pleased her greatly as she had not particularly wanted to share with her elderly relative. Though she was used to sharing a dorm with her schoolmates, a holiday, she felt, should be a little more indulgent. After the hotel porter had brought up all of their bags, Great Aunt Agnes announced that she was feeling unsettled by her collision on the platform and would be taking dinner in her suite that evening. Florence was dismayed.

"I thought we might meet some of the other residents? There is an ensemble playing in the ballroom after dinner, at least I think that's what the notice in the reception said." Florence tried to sound disinterested, though she craved the atmosphere of a sophisticated dining room.

"We will have plenty of time to meet the other guests at breakfast. Indeed, we have three weeks here, which should be adequate to become acquainted with a number of people."

"May I have my dinner in the dining room?"

"Certainly not! If I am not able to chaperone you, you must stay in your room or here with me. We shall eat together here at the table."

It was not what Florence wanted.

Florence endured her dinner, served on elegant china at the small round table in the window of Great Aunt Agnes' suite. She knew her great aunt's routine now, her abrupt way of addressing the staff, her reluctance to try anything unfamiliar to her very British palate. Florence also knew that Great Aunt Agnes would retire to her bed after their meal and would be soundly asleep by ten o'clock. Florence would not argue with her great aunt, she would simply wait until she could hear the snores and then make her move.

Florence couldn't help but admire her own reflection in the mirrors that lined the walls of the main staircase. The gold and crystal surrounding her highlighted the shine of her hair and the blue of her eyes. She had chewed on her lips at the top of the stairs and was now gratified to see they had reddened and plumped.

The thrill of disobeying Great Aunt Agnes was tempered only by Florence's nervousness at being a woman alone. She liked to think that she could handle any awkward situation, given the things she had heard late at night in her school dorm. Yet she felt strangely exposed, standing on the stairs looking over the banister and across to the ballroom. She knew she should not dance with anyone, that would be unthinkable with no chaperone in tow. She would take a glass of champagne and simply watch for a few moments to satisfy her curiosity. It was with relief, then, that she saw a familiar face a moment after entering the ballroom.

Willie Clyde Martin Jnr, third son of a newspaper proprietor from Raleigh, North Carolina, stood by the bar in the ballroom and looked into his glass of whiskey. Though the Hotel claimed to serve only the best beers, wines and spirits, the brown liquid in his glass was not so fine as the bourbon he would have preferred. He was glum, that's what he was. This trip which had promised so much when he left New York was turning into a first-rate calamity. How his father had come into the possession of the sapphires he did not know. Not for the want of asking, but his Pa had clammed up like a ... well, like a clam on that subject. Take them to Uncle Manny in New York, he'd been told. So take them he had, and after a week in New York at Uncle Manny's expense, he was presented with steamer and train tickets to Genoa via Southampton, Calais, Paris, and Nice. His instructions had been clear: meet Signor Pescatore at the Bank of Saint George at midday, three days ago, and hand over the sapphires and the note that Uncle Manny had given him.

But Paris had been a calamity in its own right. Willie had wanted to see the sights and figured he'd have just enough time to do so. Except he'd had one too many strange green liqueurs in a club off the Montparnasse, gotten rather too friendly with a young lady in a red dress and had been followed by the two men in long overcoats ever since. If only he could remember what he'd said. That green drink would never pass his lips again, that was for sure! He'd missed his connection the next day and took another day to rearrange his tickets to Nice. He'd sent a telegram to Signor Pescatore to explain his predicament and could only hope that the Italian would be easy enough to find when Willie reached Genoa.

Willie knocked back the rest of his whiskey and turned towards the ballroom door as he took his cigarettes out of his jacket pocket. The girl from the platform was standing in the doorway, looking for all the world like a lost child. She spotted him and smiled; Willie raised his hand, got off his stool and made his way around the edge of the dancefloor to meet her.

"Say, hello again!" Willie held out his hand for Florence to shake. He noticed that she hesitated, and then only briefly and tentatively responded, letting go as quickly as possible.

"Good evening! It is so nice to see a familiar face."

"Is your aunt not with you?" Willie half expected to see the old girl suddenly appear at Florence's elbow or shout rudely from across the reception hall.

Florence bit her lip, "No, Great Aunt Agnes is feeling rather tired from our journey and has retired early this evening. I thought I would come down and listen to the band for a few minutes. It is rather busy though."

"There's a table in the corner there, why don't we sit for a couple of numbers? Can I get you a drink?"

Florence allowed herself to be steered to the vacant table and Willie grasped two full champagne glasses from a passing waiter.

"Your good health!" He lifted his glass to toast, and Florence simpered as she delicately tapped her glass against his.

"What brings you to Nice, Mr Martin?"

"Call me Willie, please! I guess you could say that I am on an errand for my father. I'm really just passing through on my way to Genoa, but I became ... delayed in Paris and arranging the connection here has been a trifle tiresome. If only everyone spoke English, eh?"

"French is a beautiful language. I am learning it ..." She caught herself, "learned it while at school in Bern. What does your father do?"

Over the next hour, and two more glasses of champagne, Florence learned of the newspaper offices next to Briggs Hardware Store in downtown Raleigh, of Willie's eldest brother who had been killed in the Great War and his now only older brother who was engaged to be married to the Sheriff's daughter. She learned that Willie had no sweetheart at home, and how he had tried his hand at reporting and printing but now fancied himself as a professional billiard player, making his income from winning games in the saloons around Raleigh much to his father's exasperation. Willie learned little of Florence's background, being happy to talk about himself.

"Say, would you like to dance?" Willie didn't want to waste this opportunity to be seen on the floor with such a beauty.

Florence again hesitated. Should she? It was just one dance, and Willie wasn't a stranger. "Yes, but just one and then I really must retire myself."

"Swell! But if I may say, you really don't need any beauty sleep."

At breakfast in the dining room the next morning Great Aunt Agnes asked Florence to pass her the copy of The Times newspaper and her reading glasses.

"These are not my reading spectacles." Great Aunt Agnes stated holding them out to Florence.

"Are you sure? Perhaps your eyes are more tired from the journey?"

"No, I know what tired eyes feel like. These are not mine, see here the clasp is tarnished silver, my clasps are gold."

Florence took the spectacles in her hand and examined them. She had not paid enough attention to her great aunt's glasses in the past to comment with any decision on the clasps, but she nodded and handed them back again.

"I think perhaps they were mixed up when Mr Martin crashed into us on the platform."

"How irritating. We shall have to look out for him and ask for the return of my own pair."

The prospect of looking out for Mr Martin made Florence smile and agree.

Willie at the same time was sitting on the edge of the bed in his much smaller room at the rear of the hotel, a spectacles case in his hand. He should have been more insistent with the girl; he had been sure that she was holding his case and not her great aunt's. He had checked as he had been packing to leave in his room, then checked his pockets and case, and finally checked the spectacles case once more before accepting that the small slip of paper and five pale blue sapphires were not contained in the silk lining. He would have to think carefully, how to retrieve the other case without arousing any suspicion.

He would have to telegram Signor Pescatore again and ask him to wait one more day. Willie looked at his watch. He would skip the breakfast on offer at the hotel and purchase a coffee and pastry after he'd been to the post office. He sighed; at this rate he would need to wire Uncle Manny for some more cash as well.

As Florence and Great Aunt Agnes emerged from the dining room, Florence caught sight of Willie's striped blazer as he pushed through the revolving entrance doors of the Hotel onto the street outside. She had hoped he would be taking breakfast and had craned her neck to inspect every new arrival to the dining room until Great Aunt Agnes had said she was beginning to look like a giraffe.

An elderly couple who Great Aunt Agnes recognised from a previous visit to the hotel joined them towards the end of their meal and Florence endured the conversation that centred on how the Promenade was not as clean as last time, how the streets seemed more crowded, and the motor cars noisier. Not realising that Florence's French was average, the elderly lady commented on how the young people were also far more outrageous than ever before. Florence looked down and smiled to herself, before a sudden stab of guilt erased her smile – what if this couple had seen her with Mr Martin the evening before? She listened carefully but could detect no specific reference to dancing and breathed a sigh of relief.

Great Aunt Agnes had decided they would take a short walk along the Promenade after breakfast to the public gardens where they would sit in the shade and read until lunchtime. Florence would rather have sat in a deck chair overlooking the sea, or spent time in the hair salon, but agreed to her great aunt's plans. She wondered where Mr Martin had gone; he had no luggage with him so could not have been leaving for Genoa. Florence wondered about America. She had been so absorbed in European culture for the past two years, and so rarely went to the cinema, that America had not been a feature of her daydreams. Finishing school was all very well, but there was still so much of the world she needed to learn about.

Willie collected a telegram from Uncle Manny on his return to the hotel which had been sent the previous day. Now he felt such a fool for sending his own, as Uncle Manny made it clear as day that no more funds would be forthcoming until Willie had delivered the items to Signor Pescatore. Uncle Manny seemed to know that there had been some trouble in Paris too, though how he could possibly do so was beyond Willie. Well, there was one way Willie felt sure he could work up a little more cash. He'd seen a bar with a billiards table on his way from the post office. He hadn't seen the men in long coats watching him from their motorcar across the street as he left the hotel and didn't see them get out of the car and follow him to the bar.

"I shall be taking an hour's rest after lunch, and then we will visit the gallery of an old friend this afternoon." Great Aunt Agnes dabbed her lips with her napkin.

Florence liked art, though she had no skill in producing any. "That sounds interesting. How did you come to know a gallery owner here?"

"Your Great Uncle Hector was very interested in art. Monsieur Roche arranged for the purchase and sale of a few items for him, and we visited him and his wife once or twice. I like to maintain the friendship; he is such an interesting man."

"Do they have any children?" Florence was hoping there would be some other younger people she could talk to once Mr Martin continued with his journey.

"His grandson takes care of some of the gallery business these days. His son, sadly, is more interested in restoration work."

Florence understood from the tone of Great Aunt Agnes' voice that restoration work was not an occupation that bestowed prestige or riches upon Monsieur Roche's son. Perhaps the grandson would have Great Aunt Agnes' approval.

Willie sunk the final billiard ball with a shot off two cushions. His opponent shook his head slowly and blew out cigarette smoke. The five Franc note that sat under a whiskey glass on the end of the bar was now Willie's, but Luc Fornier was sure he could beat the arrogant American in a best-of-three.

"We play again." Luc said as he began to retrieve the balls.

"Sure, double or quits my friend." Willie was equally certain he could beat anyone in the bar at his favourite game.

"Non. Meilleur des trois matchs. Pour vingt Francs."

Willie looked confused, "Say what now?"

Using the tip of his cue, Luc gestured at the table and held up three fingers on his other hand. Then he tapped the whiskey glass with the cue tip and flexed all five fingers four times. Willie was a quick learner; if this guy wanted humiliation, Willie would be happy to oblige for twenty Francs profit. He'd let Luc win the next game to keep things interesting and then go in for the kill.

At the end of the second game, a few men had moved closer to the table to watch. They shook Luc's hand as he stood up after potting the final ball and some slapped him on the back. The barman poured the players another drink each, and the third and final game was set up. Two men in long coats took seats in the window and ordered coffees.

The third game was close. Willie missed a clear shot and thought he had left the table wide open for Luc. Then Luc made an equally shoddy attempt and Willie was back in the driving seat. More men gathered around the table. The air was thick with smoke and the aroma of coffee. Willie missed another shot and the audience cheered as if Luc had already won. Willie noticed the sweat on Luc's brow and wondered for a second just how much twenty Francs was to the young Frenchman. Just as Luc was taking his shot there was a crash from the kitchen of the bar and Luc mis-cued. Willie took his time in chalking his own cue while the crowd settled down again. Then he dispatched the remaining balls.

Willie wanted to leave the bar with his winnings as quickly as possible. The mood had turned from jovial to sour when Luc Fornier was obliged to hand over twenty Francs, some of which were small change now chinking together in Willie's pocket as he hurried along the Promenade. Willie had also thought he recognised the two men in the window seat as he left; they had looked out of the window as he'd passed them, but their coats were draped over a spare chair and they did not have the look of regular customers.

There was nothing else for it but for Willie to lay low at the hotel until he could board the train for Genoa the following day. He still had to get the spectacles case back from the old woman, but he knew which rooms were theirs as he had escorted Florence to her door the evening before. He could slip in and make the switch if he could be sure they were out somewhere.

The gallery was a small room on the ground floor of a three-storey building in a side street. Florence wondered how her great uncle Hector had met Monsieur Roche but decided not to ask any further questions of her great aunt. Despite the large window, the gallery faced north and was in perpetual shade. Rene Roche was explaining in good English that this was beneficial, as sunlight on the paintings would damage them. He was a pleasant-looking young man, Florence decided. A little short, a little too earnest, but at least he spoke English. Great Aunt Agnes sat towards the rear of the gallery with Monsieur Roche and chatted quietly while keeping her eye on Florence and the young man. She liked what Monsieur was telling her of Rene's achievements in sales and acquisitions. There were prospects there that could be nurtured. Still no title of course, but one to keep simmering for as long as necessary.

Willie sat on the edge of his bed and mopped his face with his handkerchief. He was used to the heat of Raleigh in the summer, but racing along the Promenade in the sun and then practically bounding up the stairs to his room had broken him out in a sweat. There was a knock at his door. Willie tensed; could he have been followed after all?

"Who is it? Qu'est-ce?"

A woman's voice replied, "Service de Chambre."

"Oh gee! Sure, come on in! Entre!"

The woman was older than Willie and dressed in the obligatory black uniform with a while apron and cap. She carried a bale of white towels and proceeded to exchange the ones he had used that morning for the fresh ones in her arms. As she was leaving, Willie had a thought.

"Say, could you bring me a bottle of cognac? I know you folks don't have bourbon here."

The woman looked at him blankly and gave a slight shrug.

"Err... apporte moi un cognac?"

She nodded and left the room. Willie hoped he had asked for a drink and not to sleep in the cellar. If he was going to snoop around the ladies' rooms, he needed some Dutch courage first.

The dining room at the Hotel le Negresco sparkled with glass, mirrors, sequins and light. Florence couldn't help a gasp of surprise as she followed her great aunt through the wide double doors that evening. It was dazzling, and looked so different without the brightness of the morning sun streaming through the windows as it had at breakfast time. The room was already half full with diners, their knives and forks adding tinkling chimes to the shivering chandeliers above. Florence and Agnes were seated, napkins unfolded with a flourish and menus placed before them. Waiters glided like swans around the tables, under the beady eye of the maître d'hôtel who stood in a black evening suit and white gloves at the door. As Great Aunt Agnes could not see the blurry menu details, it was left to Florence to order their food with Great Aunt Agnes correcting her pronunciation and tutting loudly at her mistakes. They had just started their fish course when Florence saw Willie appear at the dining room door.

Willie had drunk half a bottle of the cognac he had requested, slowly falling asleep on his bed before waking much later with a growling stomach and swimming head. He washed his face quickly and swayed gingerly along the corridor. He paused for a moment as the hotel began to spin, and reached out to the wall to steady himself. He knew he couldn't go blundering into the old lady's room in his current state, he'd be surely heard knocking something over. No, what he needed was some food to settle his stomach and then he'd be able to think up a new plan.

Willie carefully made his way down two flights of stairs to the dining room. He saw Florence in the same moment that she noticed him. She really was a beauty, he thought to himself, before realising the maître d'hôtel was talking to him.

"Oh yes, dinner, lead the way, old man."

"Good evening, Mr Martin." Florence said as Willie approached their table behind the maître d'hôtel, who stopped and raised an eyebrow to establish whether Willie would be dining with the ladies. "Great Aunt, Mr Martin can dine with us, we are not so far into our meal." She tried not to make it a question that Great Aunt Agnes could refuse.

"Oh, I don't want to intrude..." offered Willie, without any attempt to move on.

Great Aunt Agnes was in a good mood after seeing her friend, and his grandson, and was inclined to tolerate the American's company for a while. "It is no intrusion, Mr Martin, please do take a seat. We shall be pleased to hear more of your home country, if you care to share with us."

Florence was surprised at her great aunt's change of heart but dare not question it. Instead, she smiled warmly at Willie and hoped he would not mention their dance the night before. As the ladies continued with their fish, Willie ordered a steak and sipped tentatively at his wine. Great Aunt Agnes noticed his restraint and was pleased by it. Florence noticed the slight tremble in Willie's hand and wondered if it were nerves. He had not seemed nervous the evening before.

As the waiters brought the meat dishes, Florence remembered about the spectacles.

"Mr Martin, you may remember when we had the unfortunate collision on the station platform, I insisted that the spectacles case nearest to me was that of my Great Aunt's. I'm afraid however that you were in fact correct, and that it was yours after all."

Willie couldn't believe his luck. "You don't say? Well, I haven't had a reason to use mine since then, but I was sure that the blue of my case was darker. You haven't... I mean, how did you work it out?"

"It was the clasps, Mr Martin. I noticed immediately as mine have gold clasps. Yours do not." Great Aunt Agnes smiled to herself while cutting a morsel of steak. She felt sure Rene Roche would be a man who had gold clasps on his spectacles, should he require them.

So they haven't found the sapphires, Willie was relieved. "I'll tell you what, why don't I go up and get them now and we can do a swap."

"Finish your meal first, Mr Martin. Florence can read anything I need to know in the meantime."

Willie once again bounded up the stairs to his room, eager to hand over the spectacles case to the ladies now waiting in the ballroom and to have his cargo safely back in his possession. The old lady had told him that she had his case in her handbag even though they were of no use to her. She had put them there out of habit, she said. Willie reached his door, his key ready in his hand. The door was already open.

The maid had already changed the towels, surely she would not have returned so soon. Willie's stomach suddenly felt empty despite his dinner. He tapped the door with his foot to open it a little further, bracing himself to come face to face with a burglar or the barrel of a pistol. Instead, what lay before him was a scene of frenzied disturbance. In such a small room, he had been particularly careful to pack his few belongings neatly into the wardrobe and drawers. His trunk had been under the bed. His canvas rucksack had been on top of the wardrobe. His topcoat had been on the peg on the door that led to the tiny washroom.

Now his trunk was on his bed, open like the gaping mouth of a large koi carp. Now his clothes were strewn across the floor; the wardrobe and drawers all open and spewing his belongings. Now his rucksack, where he had placed Great Aunt Agnes' spectacles case, lay under the narrow window where it had been discarded in triumph after revealing the items so hastily and recklessly sought.

Except, as Willie knew, it was not the quarry that the intruder had assumed it to be. How long would he have before they discovered their mistake and returned? And how could he now retrieve his own spectacles case without one to swap? An idea came to him as he began stuffing clothes into his case.

Ten minutes later, Willie perched on the chair next to Great Aunt Agnes. The ballroom was full once again with dancing guests and the band in the corner was making an attempt at a waltz.

"Completely irreparable, you say?" Great Aunt Agnes leant closer to Willie so that she could hear him over the music.

"I'm afraid so, both lenses smashed, the frame all twisted, one side completely detached. Really not worth the expense of repairing in my opinion. I feel such a cad for not looking sooner. But I'd like to make it up to you and pay for a new pair." Willie held out three of the five Franc notes, his hand still trembling slightly.

"Oh no, but that is too much! It was an accident after all," Great Aunt Agnes was embarrassed by the sight of the money waved so openly in front of her.

Florence had no such embarrassment. "Thank you, Mr Martin, we accept your offer, and I am sure we will be able to purchase my great aunt some new spectacles in the morning. It will be a chance for me to practice some more French." She took the notes and folded them into her small purse. "Will you stay for a drink with us?"

"I'd love to ma'am, but I'm not feeling all that well. I think an early night will be the best thing for me, but perhaps we can breakfast together in the morning?" Willie got to his feet.

"That would be delightful, wouldn't it Great Aunt?"

"We will see you in the morning, Mr Martin."

Willie shook both their hands, lingering for a moment too long for Florence's comfort. He really did feel like a cad, but not for the reason he had given her. Still, if he could get to Genoa and back in one piece, perhaps he could pick up where he was leaving off. He hoped the desk clerk had been able to find a taxi at such a late hour.

Florence and Great Aunt Agnes did not see Willie Clyde Martin Jnr the following morning. It was three days later when Great Aunt Agnes, now able to read her own newspaper having collected a new pair of spectacles the previous afternoon, saw the familiar name in a column on page five.

Body found in hunt for American

Whereabouts of gems unknown

> The body of Mr Willie Clyde Martin Jnr of Raleigh, North Carolina in the Americas was discovered beside the railway tracks just outside Genoa station on Tuesday evening. Mr Martin was believed to have been smuggling a number of rare gems across Europe, which are at present still to be accounted for. Genoa police are appealing for the public to approach them with any information that might aid in the apprehension of two male suspects seen fleeing the location where the body was found.

"I think we shall call in at Monsieur Roche's gallery again today, Florence," She said, turning to page six with a faint smile.

THE REMEMBERED

THEY HAD BECOME THE best of friends despite their many differences. Ralph was a middle child, used to blending in and with little expectation on his shoulders. His older brother would inherit, his younger sister would marry and move away. Ralph was free, in a sense, to do as he wished, to make his own way. But with that freedom came the knowledge that there would be no financial backing for whatever he chose. For some, that would have been galling. To know that both siblings would receive a share of the family wealth at some time in the future, but not to have any claim on any part of it oneself. Ralph had realised the situation early on. He was used to it. It played no part now in his mission to establish himself as his own man, away from the shadow of his brother and father.

It gave Ralph an easy-going air. He placed no expectation on anyone else, sometimes appearing uncaring or disinterested. Freddie knew this was not the case; Ralph cared deeply for his friends and family, he simply would not pin any hopes on any of them. Perhaps for fear of being let down. For Ralph, if something were good enough then it would do. Ralph did not need perfection, did not seek out excellence, and would not press for more.

He rarely complained yet was never full of irritating or overdone optimism or gratitude. Ralph just was.

They had been together for almost their whole time at the Front. Ralph had joined up three months before Freddie and had passed through his basics without distinction. Freddie had arrived as an eager new recruit, and quickly became disheartened at the trench digging and boarding. Ralph's quiet, calm presence beside Freddie seemed to rub off on him; that same calm quietness when they faced their first casualties, and their first night of shelling converted Freddie's enthusiasm and bravado, his revulsion and terror, to courage. Freddie would not be the man he was without Ralph's influence, and he knew it.

When they were given brief home leave just before Christmas in 1917, Ralph immediately sensed his friend's mood change. When the sergeant had moved away, Ralph folded his pass and tucked it inside his tunic.

"Two nights is better than nothing. Time enough for a good meal and some clean clothes at least."

Freddie folded his own pass slowly. "By the time I make it to Cheltenham it will be time to turn around and come back again."

"And you don't want to go." It was not a question. Ralph was aware that Freddie carried a far greater burden of expectation than he did.

"It sounds ungrateful, I know. And don't get me wrong, I do want to see my parents and Caroline, and even Annie and Mrs Monger again. But I am tired, and the thought of spending two of the three days on a train, and to be fussed over and have to make encouraging small talk about all this... and Caroline would see straight through any fabrication, I have no doubt about that.

I can convince her that everything is alright when I write, but I don't think I could keep up the pretence face to face."

"Come home with me then. We're only a couple of hours from Dover."

"Won't your parents mind, particularly so close to Christmas?"

"I doubt they will notice we're there."

The channel crossing had been rough, with even hardened sailors vomiting over the side of the ship or groaning in their bunks. On shaky legs, Ralph and Freddie had woven their way through the crowds and boarded the train to Maidstone, dropping onto the sprung carriage seats with great sighs. Other soldiers in uniform joined them, unknown but brothers in arms. They shared smokes but spoke little, each contemplating what awaited them at the end of their journey.

Ralph and Freddie left the train at the Barracks station, and walked the short distance to Queen's Road where Ralph's parents had a red brick house set back in a quarter acre of gardens. The wind was bitterly cold, but no snow had fallen yet across the south-east of England. Carts rumbled up and down the road, a few motor vans, cars and motorcycles were included in the procession, deliveries and homecomings mingled under the grey sky. At the stone gateposts marking the entrance to the Perkins' driveway, Ralph paused and touched the place where the post joined the low wall that formed the boundary with the street.

"Emma said the snow came up to here last Christmas. You'd hardly think it possible if we'd not had the same in France."

They entered the house through a door that faced to the side of the garden where large shrubs stood naked. It led to a small, dark corridor and from there to the kitchen, scullery and a small sitting room with a tiled floor and bookcases along two walls. The house was quiet. Freddie had not known what to expect, and they had not discussed Ralph's domestic arrangements.

"You can drop your kit here for now," Ralph pointed to the floor in the sitting room, off-loading his own kit bag. "You can read any of the books from here, it used to be our school room. I think... yes, here's a couple by Hardy, and Henry James if you're interested."

The sitting room had a decidedly masculine air. Leather fireside chairs with low dark wood tables stood either side of a small fireplace surrounded by dark green tiles. The green was echoed in the half-drawn curtains and lampshades, but by means of artistic contrast or economy the rug in front of the fire was an old red Turkish rectangle. Freddie could smell coal and old wood. A small clock ticked gently on the mantlepiece. It felt to him surreal; the stillness was unnerving after so much stimulus of the the past few months in France.

Having shed their kit bags and overcoats, they next reviewed the kitchen. A more familiar habitat for Freddie, the layout here was similar to the one he knew well in Glencairn Road with Mrs Monger in charge of the scrubbed table and blacked range. There was no Mrs Monger here. Ralph explained that a daily woman came in to clean and cook for the family and would not be expected before four. The clock in the sitting room had shown twenty minutes to three. Moving around the kitchen with confidence while Freddie sat on a chair, Ralph stoked the range and set a pan on to make coffee which he had bought on their way from the station. Fried bacon, sausage, eggs and bread soon followed, and the men ate without further conversation.

Sitting back in his chair and rummaging for his packet of cigarettes, Freddie realised what what missing. "Does your family not decorate before Christmas Eve?"

A hint of a smile crossed Ralph's face. "We don't decorate at all. We are Quakers. At least, Mother and Father are. John has used it to join the medical corps though he wasn't attending meetings the last time he and I spoke at any length. Emma still attends I think."

Freddie frowned, "Yet you did not join the medics?"

"I could have. I thought about it when John did. When I went to join up, no one mentioned it, so I didn't ask."

Freddie knew that the medics were only marginally less likely to be injured or killed at the Front than the rest of the Tommies. The only real difference was their refusal to carry arms.

"So if you don't celebrate Christmas, what do you do?"

"Years ago, I would have gone to the meetings. Now, there is someone I intend to visit. You're welcome to tag along."

Freddie was curious but had learned not to press Ralph. He would explain what needed to be explained at the right time.

The next morning Freddie woke late after a fitful night's sleep. He had hoped to sink into a deep slumber aided by a good dinner and even a hot bath. Yet while the bed was soft and warm, the sheets and blankets clean, dry and sweet-smelling, his dreams surfaced and woke him several times. He hoped that he had not cried out. He lay on his back staring at the ceiling for a few minutes, trying to clear his busy mind. Again, the house was quiet. If not for Emma's chatter the evening before, Freddie felt it would have been oppressive.

Ralph's parents were small people. Their movements were deliberate and measured, efficient and without flourish. Freddie found himself thinking of his mother and how she would have brought out the best china in his honour. She would have asked question after question without hearing his answers before giving him a full description of the goings on in their circle of acquaintances. His father would have contributed occasionally at the dinner table, then later would have asked more serious questions of Freddie. Caroline ... Freddie smiled in spite of his reluctance to return home. Caroline would have thrown her arms around his neck, to the stern disapproval of their mother, and would have waited up for him, curled up on his bed with a book, to tell him all her news before finally leaving him to sleep.

At least, the Caroline he had last said goodbye to just over two years ago would have done those things. Could she have changed so much during his absence? And what of Annie, their little maid. He knew she still worked for them as Caroline's letters frequently mentioned her, but Freddie knew times were changing and the young women were now looking away from domestic servitude for their employment. Annie was a sharp girl. Freddie would not be surprised if she left them to become a nurse or a factory worker. Could he imagine Caroline doing either of those things? Not a nurse, she was far too clumsy though she had compassion. Really, she had no need to find employment. Their parents would more likely be looking for a husband than a job for her in a couple of years time.

Freddie sat up and swung his feet onto the floorboards. This was John's room. John who at that moment was driving an ambulance just outside Cambrai carrying a wounded soldier away from the field hospital and towards the train station. John who had seen the Battle of Aras the April before and dragged, then carried a severely wounded soldier who had lost an ear and the side of his face from a shell crater, talking to him all the while and praying that he would survive the ride to the field hospital. Freddie stood up, scratched his groin out of habit, and walked over to the window. He had not drawn the curtains the night before and stood looking out over the rear of the house and garden in just his long johns with his hands on his hips.

Emma was in the garden, her slim figure wrapped in an old heavy coat against the frost. She was feeding scraps to the four chickens that she had just let out of their shed, her breath hanging around her, white like ectoplasm in the still air. Like her parents, her movements were economical and deliberate. Freddie knew if she turned, she would see him. He felt the cold air raise his skin in goosepimples and relished the sensation. It felt different to the numbing cold of the trenches. Emma turned and took two paces towards the house before she looked up and directly at Freddie. She stopped. Freddie felt a familiar stirring in his long johns but made no effort to move. He could not see Emma's face clearly, yet the fact she had stopped and not then hurried inside intrigued him. They stood, the garden silent and frozen between them for some moments more before Emma resumed her walk back to the house. Freddie breathed out and turned to pick up his shirt.

If Ralph Perkins was self-contained and calm, Emma Perkins was curious, intelligent and aware of her plainness. She did not mind playing the dutiful daughter. Her father spent most of his time in London at the shoe factory, and her mother divided her time between meetings, their home, and visiting the sick and infirm. Emma accompanied her mother and found contentment in the silence of the meetings that balanced the often-chaotic environment of the infirmary. Now that the soldiers were filling the beds, Emma was considering becoming a nurse. She was hoping that her mother would make introductions for her with the young doctor who also attended their meetings.

Emma took off her coat just inside the door, then carried her basket into the kitchen. She carefully took out the eggs one by one, inspecting each for any cracks before placing them into a bowl in the pantry. There had been none the day before, but as if the chickens knew there were extra mouths to feed in the house, that morning they had produced three.

She had enjoyed the evening before, more so than any in a long time. There had been talk, with Ralph and Freddie respecting her intellect, and laughter which was a rare occurrence since her brothers had gone away. Freddie was a handsome man. She had had time to consider him when he and Ralph went to smoke in the garden after dinner. She knew she would eventually marry one of the brethren in the congregation. She hoped whoever was chosen for her would be kind and intelligent like John, and make her laugh as Ralph did. Until then, she could not stop her curiosity when it came to relationships and other people's interactions. At nineteen she felt she had learned as much as could be possible from novels.

As she turned away from the egg bowl, she gasped in surprise. Freddie was standing, now fully dressed but with his shirt open at the neck, just three feet from her.

"I'm sorry if I startled you," Freddie was smiling and not at all sorry. "Am I too late for breakfast?"

Emma couldn't prevent her cheeks from reddening. "I can make you something." She side-stepped past him and took a pan from the shelf next to the range. "Porridge?"

"Thank you. Do you make it with milk or water?"

"Milk, of course. You may add your own salt or sugar."

"Are your chickens still laying?"

"We had three eggs this morning. There's really not enough light now for them. I have heard that some farmers set up lanterns in their hen houses to encourage the hens to keep laying."

"We rarely have eggs. We rarely have chicken either. Where is Ralph?"

"Still in bed. He may not rise before lunchtime."

"And your mother?"

"She is out."

Freddie had not sat at the table, instead he leaned against the edge of the tall dresser. The thought crossed his mind that he could have Emma right there in the kitchen if she were willing and no one would know. He had taken Annette that way in the farmhouse just outside Verdun, finding her there as he tried to rejoin his Company. She had been willing; she had even given him bread and cheese afterwards. He wondered if she were still there or if she had joined the flow of refugees away from the Front.

"Who are you thinking of?"

Emma broke into his memories. She was watching him as she slowly stirred the porridge and milk in the pan.

"No one. Home." He lied. It fell off his tongue easily.

"I know that it is worse than we're told. I sit with a soldier sometimes, Reg, in the infirmary. He lost his legs. Sometimes he rambles on, it all sounds so awful, but he seems to need to talk about it so I just listen. I hear the nurses tell some of the soldiers not to talk, I think they would rather not know about it all."

"It's not all bad."

They looked at each other for a long moment as they had earlier that morning. The porridge started to bubble. A door opened with a creek upstairs. They heard Ralph relieve himself into the toilet, then pull the chain. He clumped down the stairs and into the kitchen. If he felt the tension between them, he made no reference to it; he picked up a glass from the draining board and filled it with cold water from the tap, taking a gulp then emptying it in the sink and placing it upside down again on the drainer.

"Is there enough for me too?"

Emma looked down at the glutenous grey mixture. "Perhaps, if you have some bread as well."

Emma left the men to eat in the kitchen. Freddie ate slowly, trying to unpick those moments unspoken between him and the girl. Had she felt the same? Had she wanted him? Would he have acted if Ralph had not been there too. He thought he would have made some attempt. But why had Emma behaved in that way? Freddie found the simpering and flirtatious girls tiresome. Since his first intimate encounter with a woman, admittedly not a spectacular success but accomplished all the same, he found he did not have the patience for a courtship. Perhaps he simply did not have the time, he concluded.

Freddie finished his food before Ralph. "Where is it you need to visit today?" He asked as he rolled a cigarette between his fingers, then pushed it behind his ear.

"Just someone I know. He used to come to the meetings but when the War started, he turned away."

"I thought people turned towards religion at times like this, not away from it."

"People turn to different things. Help me wash these before we go out for a smoke." He pushed his bowl away and licked his spoon one more time.

Freddie was keen to get out of the quiet of the Perkins' house. It was starting to unsettle him, the way it seemed to know what he was thinking. The strange quiet of the family was so different to his own, and a world away from the noise, mud, chaos of his life in the trenches. Freddie was feeling disoriented. Ralph appeared unaffected. Freddie envied his ability to adapt to any situation with apparent ease.

They crossed through the centre of town, out along side streets of narrow cottages that became narrower and grubbier at every turn. Ralph stopped abruptly at an unpainted door and turned the handle. The door opened directly onto a claustrophobic dark room and Freddie had a moment of heightened senses as his eyes adjusted and he scanned for movement before following his friend inside.

"Len? It's me. Are you still in bed?" Ralph called out as Freddie closed the front door behind them.

There was no answer. Ralph went through to the kitchen at the rear of the house, the debris of many meals piled high on the table and other surfaces. The back door was slightly open.

"He'll be in the lav. This gets worse every time." Ralph began to stack dirty plates to clear a small space, and handed the kettle to Freddie, instructing him to fill it and stoke the range. The fire had all but died in the small black boiler. Freddie put the full kettle on the single hot plate, then opened the fire door and used a poker to rake the coals. A faint orange glow shimmered in the draft from the open back door. Freddie looked around for coal to feed the boiler.

"There's nothing to burn." He said after exhausting his search.

The lavatory door opened and an elderly man emerged, bald save for a few strands of white hair that hung down over his ears. His eyes were milky and his hands twisted with arthritis. He looked towards the kitchen at the sound of his visitors.

"Who's that in there? Alfie Roberts, I'll tan your hide when I catch you, little bastard!" He had a surprisingly loud voice for one who looked so beaten by life.

"Len, it's me. Ralph. And my friend Freddie. Come on in out of the cold."

"Ralph? Jeremiah Perkins' son? I remember you, lad." Len pushed the kitchen door closed behind him and looked in semi-blindness across the cluttered wasteland of his kitchen.

"Are you out of coal, Len? Your boiler's almost cold."

"Is there none in the bucket by the door?" He knew there was not. He had used the last of it the evening before.

"All gone. When was Marjory last here?"

"Oh, I don't know. Not this week. Maybe last Thursday. She don't come as often now. Got her own things to be seeing to." Len had not seen his daughter for two weeks at least. The detritus in the kitchen said so, even if he did not.

Ralph helped the older man into the only solid-looking chair, then looked up at Freddie.

"Would you mind seeing if you can get a bucket of coal from the hardware shop we passed a couple of streets back? They usually do it for a joey, though I suppose it might have gone up while we've been away."

"Sixpence now, lad. Won't get much for a joey these days." Len sniffed and wiped his nose on the back of one hand.

"Of course." Freddie picked up the empty bucket and hurried back into the cold street and away from the smell of decay.

Retracing his steps towards the hardware store, Freddie made up his mind that coal by itself would not help Len. He had money in his pocket that clearly wouldn't be needed for Christmas gifts for his hosts, and the sight of Len's mean surroundings had prompted an unfamiliar feeling of guilt in Freddie. He had not wanted to see his own family; he understood why Marjory might not want to see hers.

When Freddie returned to Len's house, Ralph had done his best to clear away some of the cause of the smell. With no hot water, he'd had only limited success, but had convinced Len to put on some cleaner clothes. Len was now settled in a chair in the front room with a rough blanket tucked over his knees. Freddie got the boiler going again, then set about the fireplace in the front room. Len protested half-heartedly that he wouldn't be able to keep both fires going for long.

Freddie had brought back some basic provisions, bread, tea, bacon, eggs and cheese, which Ralph turned into an omelette and brought to Len with a fork. He also bought a local newspaper, thinking the Len might be interested in the news but forgetting that the old man's eyes could no longer make out the small print. With Len sucking on mouthfuls of omelette, Ralph read out the first two pages of the newspaper to him.

They had been with Len for nearly two hours when they closed his front door with a cheerio.

"He'll be warm enough today anyway." Ralph's breath turned to vapour in the cold air and the breeze lifted his fringe.

"And for a week I should think. I ordered a delivery for him. And some more groceries too. I didn't think about the laundry though, perhaps I should go back and see if they could arrange something."

Ralph stopped in the middle of the path.

"You did all that?"

"Yes." Freddie had stopped too now and turned back to face his friend. "He needed it, clearly, and I can afford it. It is Christmas after all."

Ralph shook his head. "You've got it all wrong, my friend." He began walking again and Freddie fell into step beside him, frowning and confused. "Len isn't poor. Not financially at any rate. He owns several properties here in Maidstone, all rented out, and three shops. I believe he won those in a game of cards before he joined the Quakers. No, Len has sufficient income."

"Yet he lives like that? Do you mean to say he chooses to? Or is he pretending for some reason?"

"His sight is worse than the last time I saw him, I don't think that's a pretence."

"I don't understand."

"He lost his faith. He lost his wife, Jenny. She walked out one day and left Len with Marjory, who was fourteen at the time. One minute they were a happy family, if you believe Len, and the next his world comes crashing down around him. He made some poor business decisions, oh yes, he had investments as well but lost out in a take-over. I'm not sure of the exact details and Len revises them each time he talks about it. Marjory stayed with him until she was sixteen or thereabouts, and then married the first man who proposed. She's a nice girl, but Len had expected her to take on her mother's duties ..."

"All girls are meant to look after the home, aren't they. Your Emma does, and I'm sure Caroline will as she gets older."

"I'm only repeating what I've heard over the years, and some of that is third or fourth hand. There was a discussion with the Elders about it all. It wasn't just the housework that Marjory was expected to take on."

They continued to walk for a few moments while the comprehension of what Ralph was saying settled on Freddie. They crossed the street and made for Queen's Road.

"Len's reputation was ruined. He sold the family home and moved into one of his empty properties, and then when word got around, he moved again to where he is now. Marjory still visits, but it looks like even she is finally starting to avoid him. I wonder if she might have moved away too."

"Yet you still visit him. Why?"

"Because he remembered me. He hadn't been to meetings for a while, and I was only vaguely aware then of what was going on. But I saw him sitting on a bench in the gardens one day and he smiled at me and said hello. He said, 'Hello young Ralph.' I sat on the bench with him for a few minutes and we talked about what I was doing at technical school. He remembered me, so now I remember him."

"But still, now you know what was really happening, with Marjory I mean, doesn't that change your opinion of him?"

"I don't really have an opinion of him. I can't say we're friends, I'm not even sure that we like each other particularly. But he remembered me. It's no skin off my nose to call in when I'm here for a few minutes and see how he is. He's no danger to me."

"And you're not afraid that your reputation might be tainted by association?"

Ralph laughed. "I am no one, Freddie. I am not important."

On the train back to Dover, and on the boat journey across the English Channel, Freddie mulled over Ralph's words. Ralph slept for much of their trip; his ability to sleep anywhere and through just about anything was another trait Freddie admired in his friend. Did it come from Ralph's inner peace, Freddie wondered. They had not talked again of Len or Marjory. They had sat in the old school room and read in companionable silence, and dined with Ralph's parents and Emma once again. She had kissed him that morning, before Ralph joined them in the kitchen. He supposed it had been her first kiss. She had asked if she might write to him, and he had agreed, knowing in that moment that he would reply through Ralph, if at all, his physical responses to her already waning.

Freddie looked around the train compartment crammed with Tommies as it steamed through France. Some stood, dozing on their feet as they had learned to do. Others curled themselves into as small a space as possible, caps pulled over their faces and arms folded tightly across their chests. Ralph's words again in his head, 'I am no one. I am not important.' How many of them would be remembered, he wondered as his eyes began to feel heavy.

If you enjoyed these stories, please do add your star rating to either Amazon or Goodreads ~ and tell your friends!

ABOUT THE AUTHOR

Mary was born in Berkshire, England. She lived in Devon and Cornwall for several years, and now finds herself in the Cotswolds town of Cheltenham. Mary is a bit of a learning magpie; alongside her writing she is a qualified RHS garden designer, a British Computer Society Agile Practitioner, a Chapterhouse qualified proofreader, and an accredited Colour Insights practitioner, as well as having a BA Hons in Heritage and Landscape.

Mary loves to travel. Her favourite city is Copenhagen.

Printed in Great Britain
by Amazon

24443038R00066